The Scholarship

The Scholarship

By Lacey Madison

ISBN-13: 979-8-9959451-0-9 (Hardback)

ISBN-13: 979-8-9959451-1-6 (Paperback)

ISBN-13: 979-8-9959451-2-3 (E-book)

Library of Congress Control Number: 2026911386

Cover by Caroline Lackey

To my muse, my light, my love. None of this would be possible if I didn't have you by my side.

Contents

Chapter One

It was nearly nightfall when the cab pulled up outside the manor house. Dreary fog parted for the headlights shining on the large wooden doors.

The cab stopped right at the gray, cobbled steps.

"Here, m'um?" the cabbie said in a thick accent.

"Yes. Thank you," Armmie replied.

He killed the engine, and, moments later, opened Armmie's door.

She stepped out, somewhat expecting a butler or someone to descend the stairs to help with her bag, but when she looked up to the wood door, all she saw was the elusive Alton Tyner, stone-faced in brown trousers and a gray wool sweater—hair twined into a neat French twist. She studied Armmie with crossed arms from the doorframe, unmoving.

"Your trunks, m'um," said the cabbie. He held the large suitcase out, and Armmie grabbed it with her gloves, pressing coins into the cabbie's hand.

"Thank you again." She smiled politely, then turned to find Alton no longer stood in the doorway.

"Am I going to carry this myself?" Armmie muttered under her breath as the cab door slammed shut. The engine sputtered to life. The crunching of gravel, then silence. Alton was not coming to help with the bags.

After furiously dragging her heavy bag up the stairs, she pushed open the door of the manor. Immediately, light enveloped her, though not much warmth.

The black and white tiled interior entryway boasted double stairs to the second level. Oil painting collages stretched up parallel walls, and a simple yet elegant crystal chandelier hung dramatically from the ceiling.

"Um… hello?" Armmie called into the house. How strange. A house this big, yet no waitstaff to be found.

"Hello yourself," came a smooth voice. Armmie turned to see Alton, standing with arms crossed once more.

"Where is everyone?" Armmie asked.

"Everyone? I live alone."

How odd. Alton Tyner, a renowned scholar and heiress to the Von Tyner fortune, lived in solitude. Perhaps this is where her offer came from.

Months before, in the papers, Armmie saw an ad placed by Alton Tyner for the opportunity to be granted a scholarship to any school in Europe. Undoubtedly, thousands had applied, including Armmie. It had been her dream to attend the

University of Prague, but the tuition fees far exceeded anything Armmie could earn as a copy editor for London's Daily Inquirer.

Armmie received a most strange envelope with an elegant maroon seal. Shaking hands in the dim oil light, Armmie opened the letter of acceptance. Arrangements for transportation would be made, and Armmie would have to report on one hundred books over the course of a year, as dictated by Alton Tyner, to qualify for the scholarship. Armmie loved to read, and copy editing grew tiresome. It seemed obvious. And thus, Armmie Charon found herself damp and cold in the manor house of the richest woman in London. Or rather, outside of London, based on the duration of Armmie's journey. Far outside London, in fact.

"Where shall I put my things?" Armmie asked.

"This way," Alton replied. She at least had the decency to grab Armmie's trunk from her.

Armmie followed Alton up the marble stairs and down a hallway with velvet carpet. Portraits of aristocrats past lined the walls, when abruptly Alton stopped. She pushed open the dark door to reveal a lavish bedroom.

Inside was a large wool rug before an empty fireplace with a settee across from a leather armchair.

A huge feather bed with half a dozen pillows and a knitted duvet beckoned Armmie. There was a vanity, a mirror, and a walk-in closet. It was all so overwhelming.

"Lavatory is through those doors right there," Alton said, setting down Armmie's trunk. "Are you hungry?"

"Famished," said Armmie earnestly.

She had not eaten since she left the city, bidding farewell to her neighbor and ripping up a scathing letter from her former employers.

"I was preparing dinner when you arrived," Alton said. "The dining room is down the stairs on the left. Meet me when you have settled."

She bowed out shortly after, leaving Armmie aghast at this luxurious room. The best she had ever seen prior to a room such as this was her childhood friend Mel's mother and father's room. Her father, being a professor at Lockmore University, explained their two-story townhouse. Armmie's own father had been a bit of a lunatic, though the more appropriate term was sailor. Her mother wasted away by her window waiting for the man to come home from the sea. But his returns were far and few between, lasting a few days at a time. The stamp of coins on the table meant dinners until he returned.

After the authorities officially declared Armmie's father lost at sea, her mother moved in with her uncle in Scotland, leaving seventeen-year-old Armmie to fend for herself in their apartment. At least there had never been pressure to marry. Armmie had done all right for herself, but the aforementioned copy job had worn thin on her these last seven years. Though she could read and write exceptionally, given her lack of education, university had been unthinkable. Until the ad and Alton and... dinner.

Armmie was struck again and again by how peculiar it was to live in a house this large alone. It was practically a maze to reach the dining room, walking past marble statues and paintings, through beautifully wallpapered rooms with frescoes on the ceilings. It was marvelous, really. Finally, after getting lost several times, she encountered Alton reading a book at the dining room table.

"Ah. You've found me," Alton said. "Please sit."

Armmie obliged, politely seating herself at the seat at the other end of the table. Alton returned moments later, raising an eyebrow at Armmie's seating choice.

"What? Am I not supposed to sit here?" Armmie asked in a huff. Wasn't it a little early to be passing judgment?

Alton set the dish in front of Armmie wordlessly and took her seat at the other end of the table. Armmie got a sense of why Alton reacted the way she did. They were comically far apart.

"Shall I send you a letter to explain what's for dinner?" Alton inquired.

"I don't know that I'll receive it before the food gets cold."

"Very well. It will remain a mystery then," Alton said with a hint of amusement.

The dish seemed to be a rustic soup of some kind. Armmie dipped a spoon in, drinking delicately. The broth was delicious. Herbaceous and creamy, Armmie sucked it down. Next came a dish of pasta.

"I made the pasta," Alton murmured absentmindedly. Mushrooms, bitter greens, a hint of cinnamon, perhaps? Whatever it was, Alton was clearly an adept chef.

Finally, Alton brought a slice of chocolate cake to the table.

"Did you make this as well?" Armmie asked.

"No. Mrs. Welshire down the road makes all the desserts."

Armmie set down her fork.

"I'm sorry, Ms. Tyner, but do you truly have no one who works at this house?"

"Well, Greary is the groundskeeper, so you may see him around. But other than that, no. Is that quite all right, or are you afraid to be alone with me?"

"I'm not afraid!" But perhaps a buffer between the cool hazel eyes and manicured frown would ease the tension. Though she could not prove it, Armmie couldn't help but feel as though Alton already regretted her choice of applicant.

"Excellent. Then we can discuss your studies tomorrow."

"So soon?"

"What is your proposed timeline?" Alton quirked an eyebrow. "I believe you have one hundred books to get through."

Ah. That.

"Of course. I look forward to it."

"If you'd bring your dishes to the sink..." Alton trailed off.

"I'll wash them."

"That's not necessary."

"You shouldn't cook and clean. Frankly, it's unthinkable that there is no one here to—"

"Ms. Charon, is there a specific reason you are so shocked that I don't have help? Do you?"

"No! But I just assumed—"

"Well, don't. If you've come here to live out some pseudo-fantasy of high society, then I fear you will be sorely mistaken," snapped Alton.

Armmie gasped slightly at her tone, the sharpness of it.

"I—I apologize. I don't. I didn't. I'm here to learn. I'm sorry I overstepped."

"I will see you in the drawing room at 9 a.m."

Alton grabbed the dessert plate out of Armmie's hands. "Goodnight, Ms. Charon."

Back in her room, Armmie could not get comfortable. The luxurious, fluffy pillows that seemed so inviting now felt stifling. The furnace crackled loudly as logs turned to ash.

Each time Armmie tried to close her eyes, they would spring awake, the conversation from downstairs turning over and over in her head. At once, she stood and began walking down the hallway. Dim lights illuminated the seemingly endless halls. At a certain point, it occurred to Armmie that she didn't actually know where Alton's room was, but by that point, she was completely lost. How humiliating.

"Ms. Tyner?" she called out. "Hello?"

She kept at it, calling out for Alton to no avail. Eventually, she found her way back to the staircase.

"Ms. Tyner," she echoed.

Armmie would never make it to her room, so she slumped against the wall, closing her eyes. Perhaps in the morning she'd be able to find her way.

"Is there a particular reason you're sleeping against a credenza?" came the voice.

Armmie's eyes sprang open.

"I... I came to apologize. Then I got lost," Armmie said sheepishly, standing to her feet. Alton stood close to her. In the dim light, Armmie was certain she could see flickers of a smile.

"You'd best follow me."

So Armmie did, doing her best to make mental notes of how exactly she returned to her room. Hook a right at the mustache bust, and a left at the pantheon portrait.

They reached Armmie's door.

"Thank you," Armmie said, "and I'm sorry."

Alton studied her, dragging her eyes over Armmie's face. Armmie did not appreciate the height difference, while not enormous, certainly made her feel little under such a scrutinizing gaze. Eventually, it seemed that Alton reached her conclusion, whatever that was.

"Tomorrow at 9 a.m. See if you can find the drawing room on your own."

And then Alton was gone, leaving a rather dumbfounded Armmie staring at her shadow.

After a very reasonable time searching through the manor house, Armmie found Alton looking over papers in a file. She wore a navy pinstripe button-down with sleeves rolled at the elbow and navy trousers. Armmie had opted for a gray pencil skirt and sweater. How odd that Alton wore men's pants. Though clearly, oddities were no stranger to Alton Tyner.

The room itself had a large Persian rug, drapes and blinds, subdued red wallpaper, and large windows, as well as plush armchairs, one of which included Alton.

"I trust you found me okay," Alton said, not looking up from the files.

"Once I remembered how to use a compass," Armmie quipped.

Alton traced her eyes up Armmie's figure. There was something so... intense about her gaze. Armmie's stomach clenched, and she cast her eyes down and found a seat across the coffee table from Alton.

"What have you got there?" inquired Armmie.

"Your syllabus," Alton said, handing the papers to Armmie, "and the contents of our agreement."

"Some sort of contract?" Armmie asked.

"Sort of."

Armmie looked at the syllabus, formatted as a calendar. The classics, the Romantics, philosophy, science, poetry, foreign tales... it was quite extensive. Though what did she expect? One hundred books would have to include quite a bit.

"Breaks for the holidays, I see."

"You should be able to see your family, after all."

Of course. Her family. The one sank at the bottom of the sea, and the other wasted away in the country. Armmie smiled tightly. She flipped to the next page to a section entitled "Agreement and Conduct." She skimmed over it, and a section stood out.

"Should Recipient of the scholarship fail to complete the agreed-upon biweekly presentations and compositions, Recipient is subject to discipline and/or expulsion by Grantor pending appeals..." Armmie read aloud with a scoff. "What, are you going to beat me or something?"

"Not if you don't deserve it," Alton said, a twinkle in her eye.

"This seems excessive."

"If you don't agree to the terms, then I will have the cab driver return. There will be no ill wishes if you choose not to abide, but these are the rules. The choice is yours."

Alton's words hung in the air. How barbaric! Was this some kind of thinly veiled threat? Was she some kind of perverse debutante? But then again, what exactly else did Armmie have to lose? It's not like she had a top-dollar paying job with a loving wife and kids at home desperately awaiting her return.

"And what exactly are these... *rules*?" Armmie squinted.

"Let us not get bogged down by specifics." Alton cleared her throat. "I'd like to get to the curriculum."

Alton paused, as if half expecting Armmie to shoot into the air, yell in her face, and slam the door with a sound thud. But Armmie did no such thing.

"Very well," Armmie concluded, "the curriculum."

Alton cleared her throat.

"Given that there are fifty-two weeks in a year, minus two weeks' vacation, you will be expected to present to me two pages of notes per book, and a short presentation with your findings twice a week. You won't be given marks, but the quality of your report will be factored into whether it is considered complete." Alton looked up at Armmie, then back down at the paper. "Upon completing the course of study, Recipient will be awarded full tuition to the institution of their choosing. The course is divided into months, the last three being independent study. Recipient has full authority to quit the program at any time, but will not be awarded the scholarship until mutually agreed-upon by both parties. Do you accept?"

"Contracts certainly take the romance out of things," Armmie remarked.

"The romance?"

"I... no, I meant," Armmie spluttered. "I meant the mystique. Forget I said anything. Yes. I agree. I'll sign."

And so Armmie did. She scrawled her name across the dotted line and presented it back to Alton, who signed as well.

"All right, Teach. Who is my first author?" Armmie asked.

Alton stood, walked to a cabinet on the wall behind Armmie, and returned with a stack of four books.

"*Racing South* by Capricus, *Horizons Onward* by Foxe, *The Growing Points*, Davies, and *Code Noir* by Deluthe," Alton said, placing the books in Armmie's hands. "That should take us two weeks."

"These books are rather large, don't you think?"

"Then you'd best get reading. I take my tea in the sitting room this time of year, if you'd care to join me for breakfast."

Armmie did. How uncouth to be signing contracts before breakfast.

She had to follow closely behind Alton so not to get lost between one room to the next. The manor was unthinkably massive. Armmie wasn't so sure even gravity behaved the same in this place. They traversed through hall after hall, room after room, until they made it to what Armmie learned was a sitting room off the kitchen (that was different from the actual sitting room).

Armmie nibbled on a cheddar scone, sipping Earl Grey out of a Moroccan teacup. She overlooked what appeared to be a considerable garden, half obscured by the drizzly English mist.

"I should like to walk the grounds if the fog lifts," Alton mused, sipping gracefully from her cup.

"I do wonder if I'll have time to join you, what with all my reading," Armmie responded.

"Who said that was an invitation?"

Armmie's cheeks flushed. Stupid.

"You are free to roam the grounds as you so please. But I ask you not to enter the maroon doors."

"What is behind them?"

"As the lady of the house, I expect you'll heed my requests."

"Of course, Ms. Tyner."

For the love of all that is holy, could Armmie please remember her manners? It was as though everything she had ever learned leaked out without her noticing.

"Very well. Enjoy your reading. I anticipate your presentation, and suggest you begin with *Horizons Onward*," Alton said, "and by all means, you are welcome to join my walk—weather permitting."

And then she was gone.

The sitting room was comfortable enough, so Armmie situated herself on the cushioned bench of a bay window and cracked open *Horizons Onward*.

"There will always be the moment where sea meets sky. The briefest kiss of air and water..."

...

"Ms. Charon?" called a voice.

Armmie closed the book with a snap, looking to find Alton in a long wool coat.

"Are you at a reasonable stopping place?"

She looked at the page, practically seeing double.

"I suppose I've been reading quite a while," Armmie said, standing.

"Do you have a coat?" Alton asked.

"I do, upstairs," Armmie replied.

"Follow me."

So Armmie did.

They reached elegant wooden doors that Alton opened, revealing a dozen cloaks and coats.

"Choose one," Alton said. The tone of her voice... it would be difficult to say no.

"It's no trouble to get mine—" Armmie started. Alton clicked her tongue and grabbed a camel coat from the closet.

"Put this on," Alton commanded. Now it would be *really* difficult to say no. Yet Armmie felt herself hesitating all the same.

"Fine. Be cold or don't come."

And then Alton strode off. Armmie sucked in a breath. Where on earth did this disagreeableness come from? Armmie was enthusiastic about everything, yet something made her want to—well. No matter. She put on the coat and hurried after Alton.

Alton stood in the doorway to the gardens, tying her boots with seemingly intentional slowness.

Armmie caught up, buttoning her coat and slipping on her shoes as well.

"Shall we, Ms. Charon?" Alton asked.

"Let's," Armmie agreed.

The gardens were drizzly and the visibility poor, with squelchy wet dirt between mossy stone paths, yet it was gorgeous all the same. Tall, shaped hedges formed arches, and marble statues encircled a fountain.

"Greary is his name?" Armmie asked. Alton nodded. "He's done a marvelous job."

"He's worked for my family for as long as I can recall."

They strode in silence for a spell.

"Where are they? Your family," Armmie asked. Alton clenched her jaw, tensing.

"Where are yours?" Alton shot back.

Touché. As they continued walking, Armmie noticed a wrought-iron gate surrounding a plot with what were unmistakably tombstones.

"Is that a cemetery?" Armmie asked.

"You are so very observant," Alton hummed, avoiding Armmie's searching eyes.

"Well, what else could it be?"

"Perhaps we should go back. I'm rather chilled and should start on dinner," Alton said softly.

Take the hint, Armmie. Keep your mouth shut. She doesn't want to talk about it and—

"Do you plan on answering any of my questions?" Armmie snapped. "Seeing as I'll be living here for the foreseeable future. I feel it would not be unreasonable to know."

Alton's eyes roved over Armmie's frowning face. Suddenly, she felt petulant. Like a toddler denied juice.

"My family is dead. Their graves are in that cemetery," Alton said through gritted teeth. "Anything else?"

"What's behind the maroon doors?"

"Perhaps I will bring dinner to your room," Alton said dryly. "Best let you get back to your studying. Do read up on etiquette. It seems you've forgotten such skills."

Alton stormed off with infuriating grace. What was wrong with her? She put her head in her hands and sniffled. *Idiot.*

The faintest knock came at her door that night. She rushed, hoping to find Alton standing there crossly, but she was not. In the place was a silver tray and a cloche. Armmie sat at her desk, sliding the stack of books to the side. As she lifted the cloche, a waft of the dish warmed her nose. On a porcelain plate was a roast of some kind. Using the silverware, Armmie pulled apart the food, chewing the delicious meal as though it were completely flavorless. How utterly miserable. For a moment, Armmie thought to seek Alton once more. To beseech her. To apologize profusely. But she had reading to do. And more importantly, Armmie did not know where Alton's room was.

...

Over the course of the first few days, Armmie had to hold on to the walls every time she went anywhere to continually mark her progress. She did her best to make mental notes of where and what things went, but the house seemed to have no rhyme nor reason.

"Ms. Tyner?" Armmie asked as they sat for lunch one afternoon.

It had been about a week by Armmie's calculations, and Alton said about ten words to her a visit. Armmie knew she could get a bit more. If she had to guess, Alton probably had a lot to say, and just wasn't used to having a companion around. Why she kept to herself so much simply baffled Armmie. But then again, Armmie had mostly kept to herself too.

"Yes?" Alton replied.

She had her eyes on the paper. They were having a tomato bisque of some kind, and Alton had managed not to get any red soup on her cream sweater, despite not even looking at the crock.

"Who built this home?" Armmie asked.

"I'm not aware."

"You don't know?"

"That's what I'm suggesting."

"Do you have a guess?"

"Why would I guess?"

Her eyes were still down, still disinterested in all things Armmie.

"For fun? Or perhaps the pursuit of knowledge."

"I'll be sure to ask around."

It positively infuriated Armmie, the way Alton didn't seem to care for conversation.

"You know, for someone as well-spoken as you, you don't seem to talk an awful lot." Armmie scowled.

"Who said I'm well-spoken?"

"Isn't that the opinion? The scholar you are, Alton Von Tyner."

"I wasn't aware anyone thought so highly of me."

"You're being awfully modest."

Alton looked up from the paper, a hint of irritation in her eyes.

"Don't you have reading to do?"

"I'm taking a break."

"And why does that break involve me?"

"Perhaps you could use a break too. I mean, you've been at it for who knows how long. What could possibly be so interesting?"

"I'll let you have a turn after I've finished."

Alton returned to the paper.

Armmie huffed and stood. Fine. If that's how things were going to be. Then fine.

Armmie was being internally mauled by her own desire to chatter and infuriated by Alton's refusal. At dinners, Alton seemed a bit more amenable to conversation. Which meant almost nothing. Armmie assumed two normal people might get to know each other. *Oh, how was your day? Do you play a sport? Do you like any musical artists?* But Alton was content just to listen to the fireplace crackle. Which made Armmie feral. She wanted to set a trap for Alton, to bait her into conversation.

"This book I'm reading... it's very confounding."

Alton raised an eyebrow. She did not cease her elegant chewing, nor her gentle mouth dabbing with exceptional posture. But she did deign to move one muscle to indicate she had at the very least *heard* Armmie.

"Or rather, I think it has the potential to be confounding. I haven't yet come to understand what the purpose of the book is. This author, he doesn't seem to know either. And really, I find I like it when a novel has a direction, don't you?" Armmie asked.

"Sometimes," Alton responded.

"Sometimes." Armmie shook her head."When don't you like direction?"

Alton shrugged. "Now and again, I just enjoy the writing."

"Ms. Tyner, please don't make me beg you to talk to me."

"You would beg me?" There was something in her tone that Armmie couldn't quite identify, as if for the briefest moment, Alton was picturing Armmie begging for her.

"And I'm asking you not to make me. It would be highly uncouth, wouldn't you say? I mean, what would high society think?"

Anything, Alton. Really anything.

"I don't often busy myself with the inner workings of high society."

Armmie rolled her eyes. Fine. She gave up and returned to her food. When Alton came to take her dish from her, there was the briefest moment when their fingers brushed. Armmie sucked in a gasp. Alton didn't move a muscle in her face, but then she stared at Armmie with an unwavering gaze that made Armmie blush from the inside out.

"What would you beg for?" Alton asked. Her tone was… it was like crushed velvet. It was sensuous, low, craving. Or maybe that's what Armmie was hoping it was.

"Beg for a little conversation to start," Armmie said.

"I'm all ears," Alton murmured. Surely she had to be toying with her. Surely she was.

"Please talk to me."

"Aren't we talking right now?"

"Now we are. Ordinarily, I can't get you to say two sentences to me."

Alton still stood over her, plate still in hand. Armmie looked up at her and found the stare of her cool hazel eyes gazing back.

"I'm sorry you feel that way."

Then she was gone before Armmie could say another word.

Armmie had no choice but to follow her into the kitchen.

"So that's it?"

"What's it?"

"You're sorry I feel that way?"

"Ms. Charon, is there something I can particularly help you with?"

A sudden, overwhelming urge to bite Alton surged in her.

"No. Forget about it."

But then in the hall, as Armmie was climbing the stairs back to her room, she found Alton behind her.

"That was really poor begging, Ms. Charon," Alton said, overtaking her on the stairs. "I wasn't compelled in the slightest."

Armmie rushed to meet her on the landing.

"What would you like? Me to fall to my knees and beseech you?"

Alton raised an eyebrow. It seemed she would like that. Well, that was too bad. Armmie begged for no one.

"Goodnight, Ms. Tyner."

Armmie turned on her heel and walked down the hall. Ha. That'll show her. But when she turned over her shoulder at the end of the hall, she saw Alton still standing there, hands on her hips. She had watched Armmie walk the whole way, feline in her gaze.

When Armmie returned to her room, she had this unshakable feeling within her. What would it have been like to beg?

Chapter Two

Alton seemed to have an odd morning routine. For starters, she woke up obscenely early. Fortunately, there was no meal bell for Armmie to attend to, but it often felt like Alton would be a good boot camp sergeant in another life.

"What time do you usually wake?" Armmie asked some days later.

"Before the sunrises, traditionally," Alton replied.

"And why is that?"

"I get the most out of my day."

And that "day" seemed to mostly be staring out the window into the gardens and reading.

"What are you staring at out the window?" Armmie asked.

"I'm staring at the gardens."

"Have you noticed any major changes?"

"Not since I've been here."

"Then why do you keep looking?"

Alton turned to her.

"I find it rather curious that you are so very intrigued by the inner workings of my life, Ms. Charon."

"It's a compliment. I think you're intriguing."

"Perhaps your reading could intrigue you more."

This woman. So Armmie grabbed a scone wordlessly and sat with a book at the kitchen table, nibbling and pretending to read while she watched Alton standing with her hands clasped behind her back.

"You know I can see you watching me."

"I'm reading. Don't flatter yourself."

Alton huffed.

Armmie stood in front of Alton, who held a notepad of some kind, in the sitting room. Night had fallen on another dreary day, but the fire in the hearth crackled jovially.

"So... you'd like me to read you my essay?"

"Parts of it, yes. Whatever you feel is necessary for an intelligent but uneducated audience, such as myself."

"I would hardly call you uneducated, seeing as you assigned the book," Armmie wrinkled her nose.

"Proceed." Alton was not interested in excuses, it seemed.

"Ahem. Well, let's see. *Horizons Onward* was poetic and substanceless. Beautiful nothing. Some elegant prose, such as the line: 'tears of spray ran down the hull as the sinking ship cried from its splitting middle.' But what does a sinking ship have to do with the meaning of life? In my most humble opinion, Ronald Foxe massages himself with self-congratulatory sentences while dragging the reader through three hundred pages of nonsense."

"I take it you were not a fan."

"I enjoyed it very much."

"Clearly, from that glowing review." Alton cleared her throat. "What did you learn?"

"What I learned is that my hand cramps after one page of writing."

"Then I shall bring you a typewriter. What about the book, Ms. Charon?"

The way she said her name was...

Well, it...

"I don't know. I learned some people should not be writers."

Alton sucked in a breath. Paused.

"Sit, Ms. Charon," Alton spoke.

Armmie sat obediently.

"If we are to continue with your scholarship, you must try to learn something from each of the novels I provide. Think of it like vegetables. Perhaps they are not all your favorites, but they may be good for you," Alton said.

"Ms. Tyner, it was boring."

"Ms. Charon, so it was. Did you truly learn nothing?"

Armie sighed.

"I learned what one man thinks. I learned Foxe lived his life like a ship halfway underwater, and this novel may as well have been his suicide letter."

"And?"

"And that I don't wish to spend my whole life drowning. The protagonist could have taken his boat to shore, but instead, he watched the water rise until the whole boat sank. It was bleak."

Alton scribbled in her notepad.

"Good. For your next one, I'd like more analysis and less editorial. Though I welcome your opinion, maybe just the first or second paragraph."

"So you aren't going to cast me out or put me in a dunce cap for poor work?"

"Not at this time, no."

Armmie plopped down on the sofa beside Alton, who stiffened ever so slightly. *Scarcely perceptible, yet...*

"What are you reading?" Armmie asked.

"Hm?"

"I see you reading all the time. Since I just performed an outstanding number, I'd like to hear what you've been so studiously laboring over."

Alton chuckled, relaxing into the velvet sofa cushion.

"It's from the Roman philosopher, Alexandra Ovidius. Her work was never popularized due to her being a woman, but she speculates on whether a patriarchal government can ever function democratically."

"And what do you surmise?"

"Well, she suggests no. She ties it back to the fall of Olympus in Greek mythology and this and that."

"What did you learn?"

"I learned some people should be writers. And I wonder if she was correct."

Armmie bit the inside of her lip, looking at Alton. She was rather beautiful. Her hair was still twisted up, but her straight nose separated two twinkling hazel eyes and pointed toward her soft, full lips. Alton's pronounced but not overly square jaw perfectly melted into her neck. Armmie wondered what lay beneath the black knit sweater—no, she didn't...

"Would you have any interest in looking through the portrait passage?" Alton asked.

"All right," Armmie replied.

Alton led her down some halls, rooms, seating areas, and the like. They rounded upon a light blue hallway with oil paintings that seemed to stretch on the absurd length of the corridor.

"Portrait passage is an apt name," Armmie observed, "is that official?"

"It is official to the only living owner of this house," Alton said.

Armmie walked up to a man with a large bow tie and mustache.

"Who is this?" Armmie asked.

"Alejo Von Tyner, a Spanish Duke who married into the Von Tyners and opted to take our name."

"And this?"

"Angeline Baxter Von Tyner, rumored to be a spy and the wife of a diplomat."

Armmie pointed to another one.

"Edwin Maxwell Von Tyner, my uncle and scheming narcissist," Alton said, a flare of contempt behind the words.

"Aww! Is this you?" Armmie asked, pointing to a young teenage Alton, who posed primly in a rose dress with bows in her hair.

"Regrettably." Alton grimaced. "I have learned to love dressing for myself instead of for the world."

"Who is this one?" Armmie pointed to a pale woman with sad eyes.

"Eloise. My mother."

"She was beautiful."

Alton nodded, tight-lipped. A question lingered on Armmie's tongue, but before she could say anything, Alton spoke again.

"There are more wings of art, should you care to look," Alton looked uncomfortable now, "I find history can be quite a drag."

"Is that why you're having me spend over a month on history lessons?"

Alton grinned, then flattened her mouth to look as though she had no ulterior motives, that it was pure coincidence.

"Follow me."

So Armmie did. They traipsed through this whimsical manor, past the busts and statues, though the more "modern" pieces and the old. Alton stopped at one of a cherub in the arms of an angel. The gaze between the pair was so tender and sincere; Armmie felt a wave of calm wash over her. And an inexplicable twinge of jealousy.

"The Angelic Pair is a favorite of mine. I'm rather taken by the touch of the angel. She seems to look off as if she waits for the right moment to leave. But the cherub doesn't know. The cherub believes this moment will never end."

"Ms. Tyner, I'm inclined to disagree with you. It appears to me that the angel is looking to protect the cherub in her arms from danger."

"Hm," Alton thought aloud, "I never thought of it that way."

"Always one foot out the door, are you?"

Alton rolled her eyes.

"Remind me why I brought you here?"

"Because it's inappropriate to leave your house guest completely unaware of her new residence."

"Oh, is that right?" Alton raised an eyebrow. "Well, go on, house guest, how have you enjoyed your tour of the new residence?"

"A touch small for my taste," Armmie hummed.

"Apologies. I'll let the original contractors know, and perhaps they can do an expansion after being raised from the dead."

"Now you're thinking."

Alton strode off down the hallway, Armmie on her heels.

"You didn't even ask my favorite piece."

"Excuse my manners, house guest. Which piece did you enjoy the best?"

"I liked you in a dress. Perhaps we can get you in one for old times' sake."

"Perhaps not."

"You're no fun. Not even a spot of dress-up?"

"You have no idea what dress-up looks like in this house."

"Whatever do you mean?"

"Few clothes here are from this century."

"And you don't wish to show me because...?"

"Because this is your room."

Alton was right. This was, in fact, Armmie's room.

"Don't think I'll be letting this go."

"I am certain you will not."

Alton opened the door for Armmie, and she slipped inside.

"Goodnight, Ms. Tyner."

"And you, Ms. Charon."

True to form, Armmie did not. At breakfast the next day, Armmie asked again.

"Ms. Tyner, per our conversation—" she started.

"No." Alton did not look up from her morning paper.

That afternoon, Armmie sat in the reading room, going over *The Growing Points*, when Alton walked in. She held her newspaper tucked under her arm, hair still in a French twist. Armmie opened her mouth to speak, while Alton faced the built-in cabinets.

"No, Ms. Charon," Alton said, back still turned.

"Alton! Why are you refusing to have any fun?"

"Alton?" Alton asked.

"Excuse me, Ms. Tyner, why are you refusing to have any fun?"

"Do you not have reading to attend to?"

Fair point.

"Tonight."

"I shall consider."

Then at dinner. Alton dropped off a dish of spiced rice in front of Armmie and then found her way to the far end of the table.

Armmie didn't even say anything. She just looked at Alton. And Alton returned her gaze.

"Have you always been this persistent?"

No, in truth. Ordinarily, she had been a bystander. A passenger on her own boat, waiting to board. Perfectly content to get only what she needed.

Armmie just raised a brow—unclear if Alton could even see it from so far away—but they sat in silence, eating for a moment.

"Fine. Tonight."

Armmie clapped.

"Cheers, Ms. Tyner."

Alton drank from her glass.

"Alton is more fitting."

"I feel the same," Armmie agreed. "Armmie."

"How are you finding the book, Armmie?" Alton asked. There seemed to be some level of enjoyment that Alton felt, swishing Armmie's name in her mouth along with the wine—though something of this nature could never be proved.

"I'm finding it on my nightstand," Armmie joked, then paused, "how am I enjoying it? Not very much. It seems absurd that the main antagonist in this story is everyone but the protagonist."

"I look forward to your full report."

When all was said and done with dinner, Alton was scrubbing dishes with her sleeves rolled up, exposing her sensual hands that were not sensual at all. They were... were artistic? Someone who intended to portray an object of desire, a perfect human specimen, could have sculpted her hands, is what one might say. Armmie watched the way she dried her hands on a rag. The dampness of her fingers...

"...as you've insisted."

What was Alton saying?

"Insisted. Yes, I have. And I look forward to trying them on."

Armmie sincerely hoped that was what Alton had just been talking about.

Alton sighed, resigned.

"All right, then. Let's go."

Armmie followed Alton, jubilant. They went up the stairs and straight through endless, untouched rooms until they reached oak doors.

"These are the archives."

"My goodness. You should deliver these to a museum."

"Try on whatever you please."

"You must as well."

Alton shook her head, a faint smile on her lips.

"All right."

Armmie waded through rows and rows of capes and tunics and hats and jewels. She decided her first outfit to be opulent. She found a fur coat, a feathered hat, large pearls, and a satin gown, and went back to the entrance to find Alton in striped pantaloons and a frilly shirt with a long velvet cape and saber.

"You look dashing," said Armmie.

"You look radiant," Alton replied.

"Let us trade outfits."

"What?"

"Go on. I'd like to try on your outfit and see you in mine."

Alton merely rolled her eyes.

"I'll turn around!" Armmie pressured. "I insist."

Alton went behind a row of clothes on a rack to change. Armmie wrestled her way out of the gown. There was a voyeuristic sense in the air for the briefest moment. It felt as though Alton was watching her undress. How embarrassing for Alton to see her like this, the very first time they undressed together. Which was not weird or unusual for friends or companions to do, might she add.

"Bring me the clothes," Alton said from behind the rack. Armmie obliged, noting there was, in fact, a slit between the hanging garments. They swapped, each ignoring the other's bodies out of pure respect and nothing else.

Alton stepped out in the large gown. It looked all wrong in all the right ways.

"Let us have an oil painting done for you. Your betrothed from another land will be delighted to find out his bride-to-be has beauty and a sizable dowry," Armmie jested.

"He?" Alton snorted. "There will be no husband for me."

"I understand. My parents won't be pushing for my engagement anytime soon. But do you truly believe you will never find love?"

"I feel it is rather unlikely I do. But it will never be a man, should I decide to pursue another long-term relationship."

Another? Never a man?

Armmie bowed before she could ask a question she regretted.

"You look sublime, Armmie."

"Dare I ask, is the elusive Alton Von Tyner enjoying dress-up time?"

"Try on something else," Alton said, with a hint of amusement.

Armmie was just getting used to having fabric between her legs. The pants were odd, by virtue of the style (pantaloons) and the concept (not a dress).

Armmie found an intricate, lovely white dress. She pulled it off the rack. It appeared to be a wedding dress. Slipping it on, Armmie also grabbed a tiara and scepter for good fun. Then she strutted out to see Alton in a decorated soldier's uniform. Alton's face fell.

"What? What is it?" Armmie suddenly felt terribly insecure.

"That is my mother's wedding dress."

Armmie's heart sank.

"Alton, I... I had no idea. I'm sorry."

"You look beautiful," Alton said, "but if you could take it off."

"Yes. Yes, of course."

Armmie quickly changed back into the outfit she had come in wearing.

"Alton," Armmie said upon returning to the entrance where Alton stood, already having donned her previous clothes, "I hope I didn't..."

A cold, polished face of marble replaced the slight amusement.

"You did not know, Ms. Tyner. It is no fault of your own. I should not have let us..." Alton exhaled, with a shake of her head. "I bid you goodnight."

Alton began walking down the hall to who knows where, and Armmie let her go.

Armmie sat in her bed, once more unable to sleep. How exhausting, this constant tripping over herself and upsetting Alton. At a certain point, wouldn't Alton just cry "enough" and force Armmie out? She needed to get her flippancy under control. But then again, was it really her fault that Alton got upset about everything? It seemed the woman liked measured fun in short bursts, and then immediately tired of it, unbeknownst to Armmie, who could have fun for more than ten minutes. She tossed and turned, as she often did after an evening with Alton. She couldn't seem to get herself under control. It was madness.

She looked at the sky and noticed faint puffs of smoke rising into the atmosphere. Armmie clambered to the window to find Alton, leaning against the balcony, smoking a cigarette.

Before she even knew it, Armmie had rushed downstairs in nothing but a thin nightgown and slippers into the frigid evening air.

Alton turned around, having finished the cigarette, when surprise lit her face.

"Regrettably, I just finished my smoke, but there is a pack and matches on the counter inside."

"I'm not here to smoke," Armmie said. She didn't know exactly what she wanted to say, but here goes nothing.

"I'd like to apologize for my missteps. And doing things that upset you. It's not my intention, I hope you know. I'm just trying to find my place here with you and... well... you seem a little sensitive," Armmie spluttered.

Alton raised a brow.

"I seem sensitive?"

"If not sensitive, then easily upset," Armmie corrected, as if that wasn't the same thing.

"This is quite an apology."

"Alton! I'm serious. I don't want to keep offending you, but I don't know what not to do."

"We can take our meals and discuss your work. Anything else is unnecessary."

"Have you considered that over the course of a year, perhaps I'd like a little more companionship than just meals and work?"

"What else is there to do?"

"Live a little, to start."

"Are you suggesting I'm not living?"

"Well, are you?"

"If our lives look different, do you feel it is reasonable to accuse me of some wrongdoing?"

"Ugh! Are you deliberately misinterpreting what I'm saying?" Armmie huffed.

A wry smile formed in the crook of Alton's lips.

"Perhaps."

Alton looked Armmie over, who had begun shivering in the cold.

"Let us go inside. Perhaps a tea would help us both think more clearly."

A kettle was on the stove shortly after. Armmie still felt the chill in her bones. Alton looked disapproving. About what, Armmie was not so sure.

"Per the contents of our agreement, there is no clause regarding companionship."

"It can be unofficial."

"What are the terms?"

"I will watch my tongue, provided you communicate what not to say and do. In exchange, you will not act so begrudged and disagreeable when I suggest activities or conversation outside of work and meals."

"Have I been begrudging? I don't believe so," Alton said, retrieving the boiling kettle and pouring tea for the pair.

Armmie stood with her hands on her hips.

"I'd say."

"Fine, Ms. Charon." Alton handed her a cup. "Let us shake."

She extended her hand; Armmie supplied her own. They shook.

"Your hands are cold," observed Alton.

Alton's hands were warm. They were so damn warm; Armmie half floated into a dream of being embraced in those hands, like the cherub by the angel.

"Hopefully, the tea will warm me."

"Yes, hopefully," Alton murmured.

Only then did Armmie realize Alton had been staring at her body beneath the all-too-thin nightgown. For a flash, only a flash, it seemed Alton was feasting on the silhouette of Armmie, using her imagination to underdress her, to pin her down. Or perhaps that was Armmie's wish. Either way, they both looked apart.

"If I bid you good night, are you going to chase me down once more?"

"Only if you want me to." Armmie grinned.

Alton chuckled, though for a moment Armmie could have sworn Alton's eyes were asking for the challenge.

"That won't be necessary. Good evening, Armmie."

Then Armmie went to bed.

The days following, Alton had more or less adhered to her end of the bargain. Alton bravely said and did things that perhaps other people her age might find boring or uneventful; for example, she turned on the radio. It seemed she had taken up drawing, though Armmie couldn't say for sure if that was something young people were particularly enthused about. It was better than taking a stroll around the garden and reading the paper before reading a book. Her work ethic was impressive. She was a renowned scholar, after all, specializing in philosophies and religions of the world. Though in Armmie's opinion, she was still buttoned up to the throat when it came to personal conversations. That would come eventually, like shoveling a frozen-over pathway with a teaspoon or plucking a hen one feather at a time.

Before the evening's lessons, Armmie took a stroll through the garden, one that Alton had declined to go on. She saw a gruff man turning a corner with a massive hedge shear thrown over his shoulder.

"Greary?" Armmie called after him.

He turned to face her.

"Alton? You gone and shrunk yarself?"

"I'm Armmie, Mr. Greary. I'm pursuing the scholarship with Ms. Tyner," Armmie said politely. She had almost forgotten her manners altogether, what with putting her energy into irritating Alton.

"Ah. So you are."

"Well, you've done a marvelous job cultivating this garden. I cannot wait to see it in full bloom."

"Should be quite nice, methinks."

He turned to leave.

"By the by, Mr. Greary, how long have you known the Von Tyner's?"

"Woo, my word," he whistled, "been me whole life. I was a dear friend of her father's. Shame about what happened to them."

"What did happen?"

"She hasn't told ya?"

"No, sir."

"Not my story to tell, I'm afraid." Greary adjusted the clippers. "But ya can check the papers. Biggest stories in town for weeks."

"Yes, but —"

"Nice to meet ya, Military."

"It's Armmie."

"Off ya go, Navy." Greary chuckled, then jaunted away.

The rest of her walk was puzzling. Why had Alton not told her yet? Did she not trust her? Was there some grand conspiracy? What was there to hide? Alton did not seem the murderous type. Though they never did. No, Alton seemed more the type to flee rather than fight. Armmie began to return to the manor. Manor certainly did not do justice to the building. The exterior alone was boggling. Columns and balconies. A decadent facade with gargoyles and spires, and olive trees lining the drive. This house on a hill, grander and emptier than anything she had ever known. Yet Alton filled it up. She sincerely hoped Alton would have some food prepared for dinner prior to their lesson.

"... Thus, the villainous 'they' versus the innocent 'I' does a whole new take on the victim complex. Where in many 'us' versus 'them' paradigms, the in-group wars the perceived out-group, The Growing Points tosses that perspective in the waste. It is everyone against the protagonist, to their own demise."

Alton nodded thoughtfully.

"And did you enjoy it?" Alton asked.

"Not particularly."

"I would expect nothing less."

"Well, I might enjoy some good books, if you ever deign to assign them."

"It is my hope I never do something as ridiculous as provide literature you enjoy."

Armmie scowled.

"Do I pass, Teach?"

"Yes, Armmie." A faint smile appeared on Alton's lips. "With flying colors."

"Something about that sounded sarcastic."

"That is your opinion."

"You must delight in this."

"I don't know what you mean in the slightest."

Armmie rolled her eyes and packed her things. Alton did not take her eyes off Armmie, which she found strange, because in quiet moments, Alton had her eyes anywhere but Armmie. Armmie handed the papers to Alton, who held her under an intense gaze. Armmie looked back, desperate not to fold. And she could not lie; the brief moment of eye contact caused something inexplicable to flutter.

"I find I'm hungry," Alton said, stretching out her legs, "shall we have a cookie before bed?"

Armmie nodded. She needed to stop staring, for one.

They arrived in the kitchen, and Alton lifted the lid of a breadbox to reveal half a dozen sugar cookies.

"Those look marvelous," Armmie said.

"Mrs. Welshire sends a son to ours twice a week for delivery." Alton handed a cookie to Armmie. "Should you like anything, I'll place a request."

Armmie took a bite of the cookie and was delighted to find it delicious

"Mm!" she exclaimed.

They ate in silence.

"That was wonderful," Armmie said, swallowing the last bits of the cookie, "are you to retire for the evening?"

"I think I may listen to a record in the sitting room, but no need to join me."

No need to join me didn't sound like a warm welcome.

"No need."

Disappointment briefly flashed across Alton's face and then disappeared.

"Then I bid you good night," Alton said, walking from the room.

Armmie lingered in the kitchen a moment longer. Then she heard a record playing from the sitting room. She recognized that chord anywhere. Jay Brown's jazz record, Walkin' Atlantic. It was one of Armmie's favorites. She would just pass by the sitting room. No need to stay.

So Armmie walked past, to find Alton scrawled out on a chaise lounge, tapping her foot along to "Take Me Downtown"—Armmie's favorite song off the album. As Armmie lingered in the doorframe, she mimicked the trumpet, as though she had played it herself. Then she switched to miming the keys, spinning herself around.

"I see you are familiar with Jay Brown and the Gentlemen," Alton said. She pulled back the coffee table, revealing only the rug.

"It's only my favorite band from America." Armmie smiled.

"Let us dance," Alton said.

"I can't dance," Armmie said, looking at the floor.

"Then I will teach you," Alton beckoned her, "come here."

As if her feet had minds of their own, Armmie walked to the carpet-turned-dance-floor.

"Find the beat... seven, eight, and left foot step, right foot forward... there you go. Okay, and three, four..."

Armmie felt clumsy, tripping over herself. Alton grabbed her arm and pulled her in, placing a hand on her lower back. The pressure made Armmie gasp, a gasp she had to stifle. If Alton heard it, she pretended not to.

"Let me lead," Alton said.

So Armmie did, for the most part. They danced together, bouncing to the beat. Alton spun her out, dipped her, and clasped her hand once more until they were both laughing.

"Now you're getting it." Alton smiled.

The song turned slow as Alton still held Armmie in place by the hips. Armmie looked up at Alton quizzically, as if to say, *Shall we continue?* So Alton draped both Armmie's hands on her shoulders and then put both her own hands on Armmie's lower back. The tension was intoxicating.

Jay's melancholic tune slowly droned from the record.

My baby's gone and my heart don't beat no more. My baby made my heart beat in tune. My baby was my sun and my stars and my moon. I was rich, now I'm poor, and my baby's gone too soon.

Then the piano, slow and sad.

Armmie looked up at Alton, and Alton down at her. Armmie was desperate to look away, but she couldn't. She couldn't stop staring at those hazel eyes, at that soft face. She wanted to reach out, to cup her cheek, to lean in, and the song ended. Alton pulled away. Armmie's heart was racing.

"Goodnight, Armmie," Alton said, a twinge of whimsy in her voice.

She couldn't possibly know how Armmie was feeling. Right? Armmie didn't even know what Armmie was feeling. Alton put the coffee table back in place and reclined on the chaise as though Armmie had never been there at all.

Back in her room, Armmie felt a certain discomfort in a certain place that she had never felt before. She squeezed her thighs together, which made the discomfort better, until she stopped, and it became much, much worse. Then she took off her underwear to reveal something disturbing. They seemed to be wet with something that was certainly not urine because at least she had control over that, but she was uncertain about this certain disaster because it was most certainly not normal. What to do? Was she sick? That certain sensation (in that certain place) only intensified. Her core clenched.

To the shower. That ought to do it.

...

Alton seemed to be a stickler for routine, Armmie had noticed. Armmie, on the other hand, was not. Armmie was the kind of gal who would be more or less content with any plans, but again, Alton was not.

"Alton, I'd like to go for a walk," Armmie would say.

And then Alton would say:

"Then go for one. I'll be strolling around three myself."

And then Armmie would go on a walk at three.

"I think I'd like dessert for dinner tonight," Armmie might say.

"You should. I'll be saving mine for after."

And then Armmie would eat dessert after dinner. Armmie had this furious addiction forming to Alton. It was getting terrible. After that whole dancing nonsense, Armmie wanted to be close to Alton desperately. Desperately. She wanted her hand on her back. She wanted to be touching her. It was filth. Armmie was beside herself. What to do? It seemed nearly impossible for her not to fold over herself trying to make Alton like her.

They sat in the sitting room, reading. Well, Alton sat in the sitting room reading. A blanket covered her. Armmie walked in and plopped right next to her. Alton glanced at her sidelong.

"I can move," she said.

"No, that's not necessary." Armmie was doing her best to seem nonchalant. Oh, she just happened to sit here. Didn't even occur to her Alton could also be on the couch. Then Armmie wriggled under the blanket. She might as well get comfortable.

"Your feet are cold," Alton grumbled.

"My feet aren't even touching you."

"Yet I can feel them."

Armmie put her cold feet right on Alton.

"Ms. Charon! Could you please!" Alton hissed.

Yet, she wasn't angry so much as she was annoyed.

"If you warmed them up, they wouldn't be so cold."

"Is there not a single other place in this three-story house you could be sitting?" Alton asked. Though despite her protesting, Alton hadn't actually moved at all.

"You'll be much warmer with me under this blanket," Armmie informed her.

"I wasn't cold in the first place."

Alton returned to her book. Armmie shuffled over a little. Barely perceptible. Barely. Then, she scooted over a little more. Then a little more, until her shoulders were brushed against Alton's.

"Any closer and I'm moving," Alton warned her.

Yet, she had not budged. That said, Armmie knew when not to push it. So she and Alton read next to each other. A faint hint of wood and smoke wafted over her, much like the whispers of a dying fireplace. She found herself getting a little drowsy. Her eyes started to close. Then they closed a little more. And a little more still. When she woke, she was in Alton's arms. Alton had carried her up the stairs and was halfway down the hall.

"You're very strong," Armmie murmured.

"You're very sleepy," Alton returned. Armmie couldn't argue with that.

Chapter Three

Racing South turned out not to be Armmie's favorite, but she was rather fond of *Code Noir*. Armmie stood in the sitting room, once again reading from her now typewritten essay.

"Deluthe uses suspense like a weapon. Behind every corner is a realization that the protagonist, Violet Ellipse, can use to further solve the mystery of where her father's fortune has gone, until it doesn't. The reader may find themselves wide-eyed well into the night between twists in romance, twists of fate, and the twist at the end blows the reader away. This novel is a master class in nail-biting language and drawn-out conclusions," Armmie said, looking up.

Alton scribbled something on her notepad.

"Very well done," Alton remarked, "what did you make of Deluthe's use of the gun?"

"I thought it was an apt metaphor for the protagonist's traumatized trigger finger," Armmie responded.

"I'm inclined to agree. Are you ready for the next four?"

"I am."

Alton acquired four more books and placed them in Armmie's hands.

"*Water Lily*, Marcos, *The Broken Phonograph*, Henry, *Written in White*, Trotter, and *Glass Underground* by Abel Mathews," Alton said, "then we move to classics."

"What exactly constitutes the classics?" asked Armmie.

"I'll give you a lesson before we begin that unit, if you're so inclined."

She was so inclined. Indeed, she was inclined.

"I'd like that, thanks," Armmie said, "shall we cook dinner?"

"It's unnecessary for you to —"

"Please. I insist. You've done more cooking these last few weeks. Surely you need a break."

"I—"

"You can stand guard while I prepare something. I'm not a terrible chef if that's what you're afraid of."

Alton gave a cheeky grin.

"Very well."

Soon after, the kitchen smelled of garlic and roasted vegetables. Alton leaned against the counter, looking poised to take over at any time.

"I would think that—" Alton began.

"Alton. Please. I know how to slice a chicken." Armmie paused. "Do you seldom let others do things? I suppose not. Given all the nobody around."

"What do you mean?"

"Well, you haven't got a cook to boss or a maid to chastise," Armmie noted. "Since you don't, it has been building up inside of you simply *waiting* to give orders, or you isolate so you don't feel the need to control everyone else."

Alton's expression faded from amusement to displeasure in a second.

"You don't know what you're talking about," Alton seethed through gritted teeth.

"Go on and explain it to me."

"I don't owe you an explanation. You are a guest in my home."

"Back to this! Just because my name isn't on the deed doesn't mean I'm just some specter haunting your halls. Do you think I appreciate being told no any time I try to understand you and your life?"

"Your insistence on getting your way is unbecoming, and your assumptions are unappreciated."

"Damn you, Alton Von Tyner."

The displeasure flashed to anger in Alton's eyes, tightening her lips.

"Watch your language, Ms. Charon."

"I'll say whatever I damn well please," Armmie spat, crossing her arms, "and you won't do a damn thing about it."

With one hand, Alton turned off the burner under the pan cooking their meal. Then she wrapped her hands around Armmie's hips and bent her over the kitchen counter. In an instant, she struck her hand against Armmie's rear. Armmie gasped as her cheeks flushed.

"You wouldn't dare!"

"I'll do whatever I damn well please," Alton said, striking again. Armmie attempted to get up, but Alton's left hand pinned her down.

"Alton, stop it!"

"No," Alton said simply, and continued several more times, "and that's Ms. Tyner to you."

Then she let go. Armmie shot up, face completely red.

"I hate you," Armmie simmered.

"Don't make me put you over my knee."

Armmie's jaw dropped. Alton turned the stove back on.

"That didn't hurt, and you know it. Finish up dinner. I'll be waiting at the table since you don't want my help."

And then she was gone.

Armmie looked over the meal. She rubbed her left upper thigh. Alton was right. It didn't hurt. In fact, it was quite the opposite. That certain feeling—oh! Dinner was burning. Armmie began stirring the pan. Should she leave? Was Alton psychotic? Was this scholarship worth it? If she packed her things now, she could make it home by morning. Did Alton derive some kind of sick pleasure from *hitting* her house guests? The better question was, did Armmie get some kind of sick pleasure from being hit? Dinner was burning again. She took it off the stove. She plated it. She should go. She should leave dinner on the counter and never return. She picked up both plates. She walked the plates into the dining room, where Alton already sat at the head of the table. She should throw the dishes at stupid Alton and storm out the door. She set the dish in front of Alton, face still burning. Her ass doing the same. Well. A little.

Leave Armmie. Leave.

She sat down at the table across from Alton.

"Dinner looks lovely. And a little burnt," Alton inspected. "Did something distract you while you were cooking?"

"No. I burnt it on purpose," Armmie scowled.

"Mm. Who doesn't like a little roast?"

"You are incorrigible."

"And you are disobedient. Shall we keep beating this horse, or would you like to talk about something new?"

Armmie chewed.

"I'd like to go explore the town."

"I'll call us a cab tomorrow."

"Who said that was an invitation?"

Alton raised an eyebrow.

"You can go on your own, though I look forward to hearing how you find the town you've never been to before, know nothing of, or any of its inhabitants.

"I didn't realize I was forgiven for my transgressions."

"Rest assured. The past is the past; if you'd like a tour guide. Otherwise, I will await the report."

Armmie chewed on dinner.

"By all means, you are welcome to join. Weather permitting."

Some horrid, unforeseen circumstance had Armmie glancing at Alton's mouth quite a bit recently. Armmie noticed her lips, soft and pink. Not so plump, but very full. She noted the way Alton chewed them as she read, the way they formed a flat line when she was displeased, and the way they twitched when she was almost amused. She wanted to feel them. Touch them. Only with her fingers, of course. Certainly not with her own lips. Certainly not.

Armmie found her in the kitchen, munching on a cinnamon twist. It was the last one.

"I was saving that!" Armmie said.

"Oh? Yet I didn't see your name on it."

"Yes, but I was coming here *specifically* to take it."

"Well, isn't that a shame?"

There were those teasing lips, pulling into a wry smile.

"So long as you don't mind my seconds." Alton handed it to her.

"I don't." Armmie scowled. The cinnamon twist was outstanding. Even though she had mostly come to be disagreeable, she *also* wanted the twist.

They stared out the window, watching as the evening sun came closer and closer to kissing the ground.

"It's beautiful out there," Armmie commented.

Alton nodded.

"Alton?" Armmie asked. Alton turned her head. They were... very close to each other. Closer than perhaps either had realized. Armmie hadn't done it on purpose.

"Yes, Armmie?" Alton asked in a low voice.

Now she had to come up with something. Her head was empty. All she could think of were those lips, so unfairly close to her face. All day she was miles away from those lips, at the other end of the table, on the other end of a book report, wherever. Never so close.

"Um…" Armmie started. *Keep stalling, keep stalling.* Was she crazy, or was Alton leaning in? Her breath caught in her throat. She stretched out onto her tiptoes as if to meet Alton's lips, when Alton turned back out the window.

"You'll remember if it was important," Alton said, then strode out of the room.

Armmie had to take a cold shower. It was terrible, but it got the miserable feeling of desire out of her system. She was chattering by the time she got out. Armmie hoped she would be able to control herself on this forsaken town outing.

The cab pulled up and circled around a fountain in the center of town. Moments later, Phil, the cabbie, opened Armmie's door. She slid out. Today, she wore a black and white polka-dotted dress and matching black heels, hair tied in a white scarf. Alton wore a white wool sweater with a black collar sticking down, black trousers, and a black coat. They looked to be coordinating from an observant eye. Certainly not intentional. Certainly not. Alton carried a small umbrella in her hand. Hopefully, the day would not rain.

"Back by eight, Ms. Tyner!" Phil called out after them. Alton nodded politely, then turned to Armmie.

"Where to first?" Armmie asked.

"The park, I say."

So, they strolled down narrow cobbled streets that opened into a lovely park. The day was overcast, yes, but not so very cold. For Alton, it wasn't. But Armmie had refused to bring a coat, citing the fact that when they left, the sun was out and she would not need one. Closer to reality, she did not want to cover up this dress she so enjoyed. Armmie did her best not to chatter, but gravitated toward Alton's warmth as they walked.

"You aren't cold, are you?" Alton mused.

"No. No. I'm not," Armmie said between shivers.

"It's good you didn't bring a coat then, as I suggested."

"Yes. Very good."

"Because if you had, you'd be too hot."

"That's what I'm implying, yes."

"Let us hope our safety never depends on your lying," Alton said, taking off her coat.

"I don't need your coat."

"You don't?"

"No."

"So if I left it here on the ground, you wouldn't take it."

"That's right. Because then you'd be cold."

"I'm wearing a long-sleeve shirt under this wool sweater. And wool trousers. You aren't even wearing stockings," Alton gestured to Armmie's bare legs.

"Stop looking at my legs."

"I think you are taking the wrong things to heart, my dear." She held out the coat, dangling it like a worm on a hook. As if to distract from saying "my dear." Armmie furrowed her brow.

"Okay."

Armmie stuck her hand out as if to take the coat. But Alton did not just hand it over, oh no. She put her own jacket on Armmie. Intentionally, as if to savor every moment of her rightness. So very *I told you so. Ugh.*

Armmie couldn't deny, though, that the warmth the jacket brought was instantaneous. And the smell. Woodsy, with a hint of smoke.

"Are you going to keep sniffing my jacket or shall we continue?" Armmie flushed.

Alton missed nothing.

So they walked. Through the sculptures in the park, others promenaded by fountains and sports pitches. Then they walked past shops and stores of trinkets and artwork. At one point, a gust of cold air brought a spot of rain, and Alton and Armmie ducked under a covered alleyway. The sun had begun setting, and cold crept in. Under the awning, Armmie and Alton stood close—for warmth—waiting for the gusts to pass. Eventually, it seemed to calm a bit.

"Dinner?"

"Let's."

So they walked into the first tavern they could find. Immediately, a roaring wood fire oven and a guitarist in the corner greeted them. The Maître d sat them in the window, where they could watch raindrops race each other to the curb. The waitress followed shortly after.

"A shepherd's pie for me, and for the lady, the fish and chips. And we'd like a bottle of the house red, if you please," Alton said.

"How did you know I wanted the fish and chips?" Armmie asked.

"Lucky guess."

That didn't sound likely, but… maybe there could be one evening where Armmie wasn't deliberately obtuse and/or argumentative.

"I'll answer one question of yours honestly if you answer one of mine," Alton said.

"Seriously?"

"Seriously."

"What's behind the maroon doors?"

Alton exhaled.

"Anything other than that."

"That's what I want to know."

"How about this? I'll owe you that answer in the future and answer another question now."

"And why would I do that?"

"Because then you get two answers. One now, one later."

"Fine. When do I get that answer?"

"When I'm ready."

Armmie huffed.

"Fine. How did your family die?"

"Influenza, assassination, suicide, and suicide."

At that very moment, the waitress dropped off their dishes.

"Anything else, loves?"

"Not at the moment." Alton smiled, as if she hadn't just said something crazy.

"Wait, hold on. Who died of what and...?"

"My turn. In your application essay, you wrote that love was a cat that, if you chased it, would never love you back. Why did you say that?"

She remembered Armmie's application papers? Armmie scarcely did. Scarcely remembered who and what she was when she wrote them. Armmie paused. She supposed she should be honest.

"I don't think anyone has ever loved me. Not my parents, nor any friends ever said anything about love. I used to pine for love, follow it around. But I just thought maybe if I let the cat go, it might one day find me. That I wouldn't have to force someone to love me."

Her words hung in the air. Oh, why had she said that? She should have lied. It was a cute metaphor! It was a silly turn of phrase! Not some overly indulgent pity-fest.

"My brother died of influenza when he was twelve. My father was killed by his brother for the fortune, and he then died of influenza. My mother killed herself. And so did my sister."

"My father sailed out of the docks one night, despite storm warnings. We found the ship he took smashed against rocks two months later."

"And your mother?"

"Gone before she ever left."

Alton ate some of her pie thoughtfully.

"And then you were alone?"

"And then I was alone."

Armmie looked at Alton. Alton held her gaze. The rain picked up harder.

"Are you going to hit me again?"

"Only if you want me to."

A glint flashed in Alton's eyes. So this was a game.

"Why would I want you to?"

"Ah. You're out of questions." She dabbed the corner of her mouth with a napkin and checked her wristwatch.

"My, would you look at the time? Phillip will be here any moment," Alton said, pulling out her wallet and depositing two large bills on the table. "That should about cover it."

"I left my wallet at the house! I will pay you back."

Alton chuckled, putting out her elbow for Armmie to grab. Armmie obliged, though it was strange to be touching someone, anyone, in such a formal fashion, let alone *Alton.*

When they exited the restaurant, Armmie dropped her hands. It was improper for her to be doing this. Improper. It would lead to feelings she couldn't control, and by the by, wasn't Alton in a position of power? Wasn't it inappropriate to be fraternizing with...

The rain picked up tremendously, and Alton opened her umbrella.

"You will not insist on standing in the rain, will you?"

"So what if I do?"

"Ever the contrarian. Fine. But give me back my coat. I don't wish to get it wet."

Armmie did. As soon as the coat slipped off one arm, the chill bit at her exposed skin. Alton observed her closely, watching each inch of skin revealed from the warm black coat when—

"Fine. You've made your point."

Armmie slipped the coat back on and stepped under the umbrella. They walked in tandem toward the fountain, where they would wait for Phil to pick them up, peering for a pair of headlights to flash through the dark night. Though it would be hard to see, really, due to the rain.

Armmie and Alton stood side by side, shoulders touching. Unthinkingly, Armmie turned to face Alton. Unthinkingly, Alton did the same. They stood now, face-to-face, as rain fell around them on all sides. The poignant splatters of water on cobblestone were a thunderclap compared to the stillness between the pair. Their breaths short. Shallow. Desperate. Alton looked down at Armmie. At her eyes, at her lips. Armmie looked up at Alton. At her eyes. At her lips, the lips that came closer to hers, until she closed her eyes and felt a gentle caress of Alton's mouth on hers. It was electric. And heavenly. It was peace, and it was fire.

Alton put her hand on the small of Armmie's back once more, pulling her in, causing a little gasp to slip out. Alton drank it in like smoke. Armmie cupped her face, desperate to keep kissing her. The softness of her lips was, to Armmie, the greatest proof of divinity she had ever known.

Then a horn beeped twice. Phillip had arrived.

Chapter Four

After their fated kiss, they mutually agreed that intimacy between grantors and recipients was inappropriate. Both Alton and Armmie hesitated after the agreement, as if hoping the other would call their bluff. But neither did, so they returned their relationship to "normal"—whatever that meant.

Days passed until one morning, Armmie realized it was her birthday. And for some reason, she had forgotten. But when Alton set down her paper on the table and went to stare out the window like a crone or a blind dog looking for the light, Armmie saw the date.

"Oh!" she remarked.

Alton turned around.

"Oh?"

"It's... it's my birthday today," Armmie replied.

"You should have said."

"I've been so busy. I've scarcely looked at a calendar in weeks."

"Well. If you read the paper, perhaps you would be more aware."

"Yes, well, I'd like to think I'm not yet so geriatric that I take my paper and coffee while contemplating my own demise."

"Is that a dig, Ms. Charon?"

"No, it's an opinion."

"It seems the opinion was rather pointed." Alton hummed. "However, I'm willing to overlook it, seeing as it is a special day."

"Will I have to give a report tonight?"

"Oh, yes."

Armmie groaned.

"Can I please do it tomorrow?"

"Present your case."

"Um... okay... well. Exhibit A. On my birthday, I don't want to. Exhibit B... I can do it tomorrow, and it will still be done. Exhibit C... I must celebrate, and I can't very well do that if a book report eats my evening up."

Alton tapped her chin.

"Hm. Compelling. And if I allow this, you commit that you will not ask for another report to be pushed, barring extenuating circumstances?"

"I only have one birthday a year."

"Very well. Your request has been approved."

"Good show, Alton!"

"What would you like to do on this day?"

"Well..."

She actually had no idea. Not only had she not celebrated a birthday meaningfully in perhaps her entire life, but she didn't have any other friends, and didn't know what there was to do around here.

"Do you have any suggestions?" she asked.

"I fear any outdoor activities, such as hiking, may be unpleasant." Alton looked at the window at the windy sleet outside. "I could take you shopping?"

"You would go shopping?"

"Or we could go to a museum."

"Why not both?"

"You are very greedy, Ms. Charon."

"And you are so very generous, Ms. Tyner."

She huffed air out of her nose, amused.

"Go get dressed."

"Dressed? I am dressed."

Alton roamed her eyes over Armmie. She raised an eyebrow. Then Armmie looked down at her pajamas. Right.

"I will return promptly," Armmie said.

She fixed her hair in the mirror of her room and put on a dark red dress with stockings and a camel coat.

When she returned downstairs, she was delighted to find Alton in a tan coat and a dark red sweater.

"Well, one of us is going to have to change," Armmie said.

"It won't be me, birthday girl. I've already called Phillip."

Alton sat in the backseat with Armmie, looking ahead. Fortunately, the rain had stopped, but the chill persisted. The nearest city was Birmingham.

"Didn't we just go out?" muttered Alton.

"I'm terribly sorry for asking you to leave the house more than once this month," Armmie replied.

Alton just rolled her eyes, but when Phillip slowed to a stop, she immediately slid out of the car. *How odd*, thought Armmie. But before she could ponder it further, she realized Alton was holding the car door open for her.

"That's hardly necessary," Armmie said.

"I believe you are looking for 'thank you.'"

The shops in Birmingham were teeming with people. It seemed that after days of rain, the denizens of the city were desperate to get outdoors.

Alton first purchased Armmie a hot chocolate. She then declined her own, saying it was too sweet. To which Armmie responded by saying she would think pickle water was too sweet. And then Alton responded by saying that cucumbers were fruits, making the pickling liquid a fruit juice, and thereby too sweet. Armmie just rolled her eyes. The hot chocolate was great, though.

They stopped into a shop with little carved stone statues. Owls, exotic animals, mystical creatures, elves, anything a heart might desire could be found in Statues and More—aptly named. There were birdhouses on the wall and an array of clocks.

A little statue of a cat on a pedestal immediately drew Armmie's attention. It was licking its own paw, seemingly disinterested in the viewer, but there was something so charming about it.

Alton came up behind her. She knew from the smell. She could feel the warmth of her body emanating onto Armmie, her presence pressing in—

"What have you got there?"

Armmie turned around. Alton was closer than she had spatially anticipated, finding her only a few inches from her face. Alton stepped back before Armmie leaned in and...

"It's a cat."

"It's lovely."

Armmie checked the price. Way out of her budget.

"Lovely with a less lovely price tag."

Alton chortled.

"I think it's cute."

Armmie set the cat down.

"I can't bear to look at it another second, or I'm going to sell some of my hair to buy it."

"Hair will grow back."

"Oh, look at you with a joke."

"I'm interested in finding a new paperweight, if you'll excuse me."

"I'll wait outside."

Alton smiled as Armmie excused herself. A young woman and a man seemed to have a spat outside, right where she stood.

"Gareth. I am absolutely sick of it."

"It's a bloody shame, cause I won't be stopping!"

Armmie was desperate to know what they were fighting about. She craned her neck while still attempting to remain innocuous. Their voices were rising. The woman looked absolutely fed up with him. She knew the feeling. Moments later, Alton appeared from the store.

"That was an exceedingly long time to find a paperweight."

"I am known for my thoroughness."

"And did you find something suitable?"

"Unfortunately, I was unsuccessful."

"Well. What else is there to do around here besides spending thirty minutes picking things up and putting them down in a store?"

"Let's go to the museum."

So Armmie followed as Alton led her around the Birmingham Natural Art Museum. It turned out to be more gems and trees that had been preserved with plaques nearby explaining the significance.

"Oh! They have an East African Safari Exhibit!" Armmie cried. For some odd reason, Alton seemed to lag behind a bit.

Armmie walked into the room to see a whole safari scene, with dead grass plains and petrified trees. Around the room were little niches that had taxidermied animals living out scenes for eternity. One of the zebras drinking from a fake watering hole, another of lions over a fake carcass. It was extremely strange.

"Yikes," was all Armmie could say.

Alton looked off. Pale. Green. Woozy. Very off.

"What do you think, Alton? Shall we safari?" Armmie joked.

"I'm..." Alton's chest looked tight, her breathing short, "I'll..."

"What, are you afraid of the elephant in the room?"

Alton said nothing. She was looking frantically for the nearest exit.

"Hey, hey. Let's get out of here. I'm not terribly fond of stuffed animals." Armmie put her hand on

Alton's back. She stiffened further, like Armmie just poured cold water down her sweater.

Outside the museum, the sky had darkened significantly, as if it were going to rain. Alton looked like an antelope in headlights.

"Alton, what's going on?"

Silence.

"Alton?"

Silence. Armmie moved in front of Alton's face.

"Alton. You're freaking me out."

She caught Alton's gaze. But Alton was not home. She needed to do something drastic, so she wrapped her arms around Alton and hugged her. Her body was hard like ice.

"It's okay."

Armmie held her for a moment. Then the Regular Alton returned, shaking out of Armmie's grasp.

"I'm fine."

"Hardly. You look like you've seen a ghost."

Alton just blinked.

"I'd like to go home."

"Of course. Of course."

On the drive back, Alton didn't say a word. This was strange, even by Alton's standards. Why on earth had she reacted in this way? Perhaps she had gone on a lavish vacation somewhere that ended in a safari gone wrong.

Armmie attempted to put her hand on Alton's on the seat, but Alton pulled it away. She didn't even mean it like that. The rain had begun to fall, matching Armmie's mood.

Back at the house, Armmie no longer felt gleeful about her birthday and her evening out with Alton. It was no longer a charming afternoon. The hot chocolate aftertaste was bitter in her mouth. She sat in her room on the sofa, attempting to read, but each word seemed to repeat itself. Hours had passed since Alton stormed off into a dim hallway, leaving Armmie in the entry alone.

Armmie shut the book. This was her seventh report to give. Only one month into the scholarship, and things seemed to be rocky every other day. She had to ponder whether it was worth it. Free tuition, yes, but... There was something about Alton Von Tyner that Armmie could not put her finger on. She was very charming when she desired. And then tense and disagreeable, which, to be fair, Armmie did secretly enjoy. But this... This was a bit too much, Armmie thought.

She delicately packed her things. Not definitively to leave, but... but just in case. Armmie had changed into some house clothes and now regretted her decision. Hopefully, she would not have to run out into the night. Phillip did not live on the premises.

Armmie headed downstairs, on guard. Something smelled good, to the credit of Ms. Alton Tyner.

She entered the kitchen, the words, *Perhaps we should terminate our contract* on her tongue, when she saw a birthday cake sitting on the table. Alton had her sleeves rolled up and a frilly, rose-printed apron on.

"Oh! You weren't supposed to see this," Alton said. She had clearly made a recovery of some kind. "Is it too late to send you back to your room?"

Armmie shrugged. *Terminate. Perhaps we should... Perhaps. Perhaps we should.. terminate...*

"Go sit, please," Alton said, grabbing the cake on the table and whisking it away.

Armmie sat, a mouth full of words banging on her teeth to get out. Alton set down a dish in front of her.

"It's a rosemary crème fresh on sage and Brie baguette, course one."

She sat down across from Armmie.

"Wow," said Armmie.

"I hope you're hungry. This is one of four."

"Oh."

Alton took her first bite. Armmie didn't eat.

"Armmie?"

Armmie looked at her.

"Are you all right?"

Armmie shrugged. *Perhaps we should...*

Alton set her fork down.

"Armmie. I... I am sincerely sorry if I ruined your birthday."

Armmie shrugged again. She couldn't quite trust herself to speak, either for fear of her eyes leaking, which would be horribly embarrassing, or for the word perhaps to jump off her tongue.

Alton stood. She walked the length of the table and sat next to Armmie. This was the first time they had sat this close together at a meal. Armmie felt silly for choosing a seat so far away from Alton that first night.

Armmie looked down. Terminate.

Alton lightly took Armmie's chin in her fingers and tilted her head up.

"Armmie..."

Armmie gazed up at her. The look in Alton's eyes just about damn near made her heart burst. Alton looked afraid.

"I'm sorry," Alton whispered. Armmie opened her mouth to speak. *Perhaps... perhaps we should ...*

"Why did you react like that? It was just a museum," Armmie choked out. Not exactly what she meant to say, but whatever. Alton sucked in a sharp breath.

"I don't like... stuff like that."

"What, taxidermy?"

There was an unplaceable look in Alton's eye with the word.

"It just creeps me out."

"I understand. But you could have just said something."

"I know. I don't know what came over me."

"Alton... Perhaps..."

"Wait. Hold that thought."

Alton bolted up from the table and returned moments later. She returned with a wrapped box in her hand.

"Go on. Open it."

With hesitation, Armmie unwrapped the box. In it was the little statue of the cat on the pedestal.

"It's darling," said Armmie.

"So you don't have to keep chasing the cat," Alton said. Her face was kind, pure. Her face was freshly fallen snow. The first bloom on a rosebush. *Oh, Alton.* Armmie needed to muster up the words to speak. The silence had gone on for a bit too long.

"Do you hate it?" she asked.

"I love it. It's very sweet, Alton. Thank you," Armmie replied.

Well, there goes that plan. Alton grinned.

"Armmie, I am truly sorry for my behavior. Hopefully, I can make it up to you with the next three courses."

So, Armmie ate her hesitations with dinner. To be fair, it was absolutely delicious. By the time Alton had cut her a slice of the cherry Chantilly cake, Armmie needed to be rolled from the table. Alton had cleared her dishes, and Armmie could hear running water as Alton cleaned them. So much for terminating the contract.

Armmie stood in the doorway, looking at Alton's impossibly straight posture. Even from behind, Alton looked marvelous. There was such an attractive air about her. Armmie felt like a bee to a flower.

"Are you watching me?" asked Alton, not turning around.

"No..."

Alton looked over her shoulder, trying to tamp down a wry smile. She dried her hands and stacked the last of the dishes. For the life of her, Armmie couldn't seem to get used to the idea of someone of this status washing a mountain of dishes.

"Armmie?" Alton asked, now leaning against the counter, a hint of hesitation in her voice.

"Yes, Alton?"

"Can... can I hug you?"

That was the absolute last thing Armmie was expecting. She probably would have presumed Alton to break out into fluent Russian before that.

Armmie nodded. Alton took swift strides to reach her and enveloped her in her arms. Oh. This. She rested the side of her face against Armmie's head, cradling her in her arms. No. Armmie couldn't leave this. It would be like leaving a fire to stand in the cold. Like leaving the table before dinner. She lay her head on Alton's chest.

"This is a friendly hug, right?" asked Armmie.

"A birthday hug," said Alton. And then she hummed "Happy Birthday."

The days following, Alton seemed entirely measured and regulated once more. Armmie placed the cat on her desk and looked at it often as she finished and presented her seventh report. What had happened, Armmie could not say. What's worse, she had hoped the event would make her care less about Alton. But the contrary seemed to be true. Now, would she be getting another birthday hug? Likely not for another year. If they even still knew each other.

Armmie was clacking away on her typewriter about *The Broken Phonograph* when she realized from her bedroom window that the sun had come out. She stood up, mid-sentence, which roughly came out to "what makes the soirée so raw is its unbound connection to—"

She was downstairs moments later. She shed her sweater, though it was still cold this time of year; the blessed sun gleamed on her skin.

"Flashing the sky, are we?" Alton's voice came from behind.

Armmie whipped around to see Alton walking jovially toward her. Today, she wore cotton trousers and a relaxed button-up shirt, revealing an angel pendant necklace hanging between her collarbones.

"I've forgotten how good it feels," Armmie said absentmindedly.

"How is the novel?" Alton asked.

"You'll find out later, won't you?"

"I suppose I will."

"Shall we see a show? Tonight?"

"And will that be before or after you complete your presentation?" Alton said with a raised eyebrow.

"After, obviously."

"I will think about it."

"You can't very well trap me here. If I want to go, I will."

"I have no doubt in my mind. In the meantime, perhaps bring the typewriter outside. I can fetch a blanket and some sandwiches."

The clouds morphed into shapes, sharply contrasted by the clear blue sky. Although it wasn't warm, their clothing suggested they might have been in a desert. Alton returned with a gingham blanket and a tray of cucumber sandwiches.

Armmie returned with a notepad, pen, and half-typed notes.

"You aren't going to write your essay half by hand, are you?"

"Why not? The rules don't specify it has to be one or the other," Armmie returned.

"So they don't."

Alton offered her a sandwich, which Armmie gracefully accepted. It was delicious, as all things Alton were. All the things she cooked.

They lay upon the blanket, looking at passing clouds. Not doing work, notably.

"I think it looks like a dog with a fishtail," Armmie remarked of a particular dog and fishlike cloud.

"I've never seen such a thing," Alton said.

"Well, now you have. Congratulations."

They lay in silence. Clouds like hazy memories floated along, blending and mixing and fading. They disappeared like words left unsaid, vanishing before they were truly formed. The sky above turned from light to dark. Good that the sandwiches were already cold, for they lay uneaten beside the two young women who were doing everything in their power not to ruin the moment. Trying to prove to the other that they were fine with the arrangement. They didn't wish to be scooting closer. They were content just to watch the passing clouds, but an unscratchable itch gnawed at them, demanding more. A slight irritation. A minor discomfort. No, the sky was enough. The sun languidly setting beneath the trees around the manor's perimeter was enough. The moment was enough. Alton wanted nothing more. Armmie wanted nothing more. Probably.

...

"Incomplete?" muttered a displeased Alton in the sitting room that night.

"I was with you all day!"

"An excuse does not excuse the result."

"So let it slide."

"Ms. Charon, do you understand that if I just 'let slide' every transgression or missed project, you would have your way entirely?"

"I don't see what's so wrong about that."

"Our agreement was 100 books," Alton chastised.

"And I'll do it tomorrow."

"You will do it tomorrow, and you'll face the consequences tonight."

"Consequences? We're not playing this game again, are we?"

"I assure you, Ms. Charon, it is not a game."

"Alton! I will do it tomorrow. I'll do it tonight if you want."

"It will not count as complete until it is done. But per the terms of our agreement, lateness is not permitted."

"I'm sorry, okay?"

"I don't believe you," Alton said, rolling up her sleeves. "Now put your hands on the desk."

"What?"

"You're a smart girl. You can do it."

There was something so smug, so patronizing in her tone. It was candy, a lollipop she was sucking on with each word.

Armmie found she would not get out of this. And some part of her, a part of her she couldn't seem to control, put her hands on the desk behind where Alton stood. She waited for the voice in her head to tell her to run. To sprint from the room and never return. But it never did. Which meant something terrible. Not only was she not afraid, but she was complying. Because she... she wanted what came next.

Alton put a hand on Armmie's lower back and swiftly bent her over the edge of the desk. She then went around the desk, opened the drawer, and pulled something out.

"Alton, what have you got—"

"You'll speak when spoken to."

She stood next to where Armmie was humiliatingly hinged at the hip. Alton tapped Armmie's rear with something hard and thin and—

"Is that a ruler?"

"Ms. Charon, what did I just say?"

Alton then pulled up Armmie's pencil skirt.

"Stop! Stop this right now," Armmie gasped.

Alton ignored her. She flicked her wrist, landing the ruler sharply.

"Speak. When. Spoken to. Now, are you ready to begin?"

Armmie was already there. No point in getting up now.

"Yes, Alton."

"Yes, Ms. Tyner," Alton corrected her.

"Yes, Ms. Tyner," Armmie murmured.

Alton nudged Armmie's legs open with her foot a little more. A little breeze chilled her exposed thighs and her... well, now this was too far!

"You are more than capable of getting this work done. You are not here for leisure, might I remind you."

"I know I—"

"This novel, *The Broken Phonograph,* was the eighth book you were to turn in to me. Thus, you will count to eight. And if I deem you were sincere, we will be finished. Hopefully, this does not happen again, Ms. Charon."

Somehow, Armmie sincerely doubted that Alton hoped they both never find themselves in this position again.

"Now count," Alton purred, "and thank me."

Then she brought down the ruler. Armmie heard a swish, then a crack. Then a sharp pain radiated where the ruler met skin. Well, perhaps pain wasn't the right word. It hurt. Oh, it hurt. But it didn't feel bad.

"One, thank you, Ms. Tyner."

Again.

"Two, thank you, Ms. Tyner."

Again.

"Three, thank you, Ms. Tyner."

As the situation progressed, the discomfort not only grew on her exposed buttocks but also in that certain area. She shifted, inhaling sharply on six.

"All right?" Alton said in a soft voice.

"Yes, Ms. Tyner," Armmie whimpered.

As if before wasn't humiliating enough, now she was playing along. Simpering, sniveling, what next? She was desperate to defy, as usual, but that certain feeling was making concentration on even the situation at hand rather difficult.

"Good girl," Alton returned to her strict tone. She loved this, no doubt. Then, the swish, *crack*. Armmie jerked forward slightly on impact. That delicate stinging returning.

"Seven, thank you, Ms. Tyner," Armmie said.

Again.

"Eight, thank you, Ms. Tyner."

The ruler landed softly on the desk.

"Well done."

Alton ran her fingers over the now tender skin. It was extraordinary, the feeling of Alton's fingertips over Armmie's exposed… well, talk about improper.

Yet, for Alton to tear her fingers away now would be far worse than anything she had just done.

"Now imagine if you don't turn in report ninety-seven," Alton mused. Her feather-light touch hesitated so briefly over Armmie's... her certain area... she could have been making it up. Armmie gasped, then wished she hadn't. Then Alton pulled Armmie's skirt back down and patted it.

"Shall we see a show? Or would you rather work on your assignment?" Alton asked.

"A show," Armmie murmured. She exhaled, then stood.

"Thank you, Ms. Tyner. I'll get that report to you tomorrow. Please allow me to freshen up; then we can go."

Armmie faced herself in the bathroom mirror. What on earth just happened? She might as well have been bicycling around nude or jumping into a pool of paint. She pulled her underwear off to inspect the damage done to her rear end, noting the already fading pink stripes. Then she looked down.

"Oh my word," Armmie said under her breath.

She had done this? How could her own body betray her in this way? Well, frankly, she didn't really understand what was happening below. But it was messy. And terrifying. And so sensitive. She wanted to touch it. Touch.. Herself… in a way that she never had before. In a way, she didn't really know how to do. Her hand slowly grazed toward her … her.. Then…

Knock, knock.

"Ready?" Alton called through the door.

Alton drove both her and Armmie to the theater that night, instead of Phillip, for privacy, she insisted. More likely, she wanted to take her olive-green sports car with cream leather seats for a drive. The night was clear. When they arrived at the theater, and Alton parked the car, she looked at Armmie.

"Are you all right, Armmie?"

Armmie looked to Alton, to the tenderness in her eyes. A glint of fear shone, as if she worried she had taken things too far.

"Yes, why would I not be?"

"Because you're quiet. I don't know that you've ever been quiet in your whole life." Alton attempted a grin.

"I'm simply contemplating."

It was true. Armmie had never found herself in circumstances like these before. In a car like this, in a home like that, with a woman like Alton. Not that she was 'with' Alton, because no, they had already agreed…

"I didn't... because, Armmie, if I..." Alton sounded earnest. Earnest. If Armmie had never been quiet, Alton had never been earnest. A night of firsts, perhaps.

"I'm quite all right, Alton."

"Truly?"

"Truly. I'm just contending with new feelings."

"New feelings?"

"I... oh, look at the time. The show begins in ten minutes."

So they got out of the car. Armmie wore a maroon dress with black buttons and a black collar, and Alton wore black trousers, a black shirt, and a maroon coat. Which was not intentional. Or anything.

They strolled into the theater lobby, where black-tie attendants were ushering guests in.

"May I take your coat?" asked a man in a bowtie.

"I'm all right to keep mine, and you?" Alton said, looking at Armmie.

"I'll keep mine as well."

Soon they were in their seats. A private box overlooking the show would soon prove to be the best seats in the house.

"My mother and father loved the theater," Alton reminisced. "They bought the box."

My goodness, Armmie thought, doing her best to ignore the indubitably large price tag on such a thing.

Another attendant came by with two glasses of champagne on a silver tray.

"Enjoy the show," she said, leaving them.

"Cheers?"

"Cheers."

Then the house lights went down. The show itself was strange and extraordinary. A whimsical retelling of an old classic, *Belle of the Ball*, a young widow finds herself in court with a magical man. Singing and dancing, the show was rightly incredible. In the last moments, the widow sings over the grave of her former lover, bidding him farewell as she prepares to move on with her life. Armmie put her hand next to the armrest of Alton, whose hand had already staked a claim. *Well, I shouldn't take over the armrest, seeing as Alton was already here*, said one little voice in her head. Another said, *Are your hands touching right now?* Then she realized they were. Their hands, Alton's hand gently, ever so slightly, rested against Armmie's. Armmie looked up at Alton's beautiful face and saw a single, silver tear trickle down her golden cheek.

A whole new voice in Armmie's head said: *Grab her hand. Hold it. Hold her tight.* But Armmie could not. As the operatic, haunting wail of the soprano echoed throughout the theater, Armmie was transfixed, both by the whisper of touch between their hands and the trail running down Alton's face. Armmie readjusted in her seat for no particular reason, leading her hand to slightly overlap with Alton's. She expected Alton to yank her hand away. To politely shake her head or smile and go back to show-going, but a micro-movement on Alton's part wedged her hand one hair closer to Armmie. Were they holding hands? No. Was Armmie's heart thundering, her pulse pounding at the soft point of contact where skin met skin? Maybe.

"I must let you go. For we can never be. Now I am alone. Darling, you left me."

The new man scoops the woman from the grave; they rest their heads together, then the curtain fell, and the audience erupted into raucous applause. Alton whisked her hand away, wiped a tear, and began clapping along with the rest of the crowd.

It did for a moment strike Armmie as odd that Alton cried during this. Her family was gone, yes, but this play was not about family in the slightest. It was about love. Romantic love.

Armmie clapped along. Then they left the box. Armmie took note of Alton's arm. She desperately wanted to hook their elbows. Which, by the way, was inappropriate and not in line with their agreement. Then—

"Alton? Alton Tyner?" rushed a young man in a fabulous, rich velvet and embroidered suit. He was linked arms (jealous) with another young man in a suit that coordinated much like Alton and Armmie's outfits coordinated if they had tried to coordinate them, which they decidedly did not. Alton whipped her head around to see the young man.

"Theodore?" Alton cried. They embraced.

"This is my ... special friend... Pierre. He's staying with me from Marseille," Theodore gestured to Pierre.

"Pleased to meet you," Alton said, extending a hand to Pierre.

"Who is this lovely thing?" Theodore smirked, looking at Armmie.

"Armmie Charon." Armmie smiled, curtseying to Theodore.

"Theodore Westleton," Theodore said, "a dear friend of Alton's. I'm certain she talks of me often."

"Oh yes. Often." Armmie smiled politely. Armmie had never heard of Theodore Wesleton in her life.

"And how do you know the great Alton Von Tyner?"

"She's doing a sort of fellowship with me," Alton cut in.

"Is that what they're calling it these days? A fellowship?"

"I believe Theodore and I are in a fellowship as well." Pierre smirked.

"Well, color me impressed you dragged our local recluse from her cave," Theodore said.

"It's the nicest cave I've ever been in," remarked Armmie.

"Ha! Listen, darlings, Pierre is having a birthday bash this autumn and you must, must, must come. I know it is a ways away, but trust me, it will be a Masquerade Ball. I shall send the invite."

"We will certainly try to attend," Alton said gracefully.

"I simply won't take no for an answer. Good evening, Alton, Armmie." Theodore smiled, tugging Pierre by the cuff.

Alton waited a few moments for them to leave.

"There's no way we are going to that."

"Are you joking? There's no way we *aren't* going to that."

"Armmie, they are all a bunch of high-brow socialites. They are judgmental and cutthroat. We won't have any fun."

"You can do whatever you like. I'm going."

Alton rolled her eyes.

"Let's just go to the car."

Armmie couldn't help but be distracted by Alton's hand on the wheel at 4 o'clock while driving home. The hand that she had just barely been holding but a few hours ago. They wound up the streets in the moonlight. Armmie hadn't really noticed from the backseat how far up the hill they were.

"Have you lived in this house your whole life?" Armmie asked.

"Yes and no. My family has owned quite a few properties over the years."

"Properties?"

Alton shrugged.

"Well, where?"

"All over."

"Can we go to one?"

"Sure. After you've completed your scholarship."

"You know, I can read books from anywhere."

"I have no doubt in my mind."

"Okay. So if we were going to go anywhere, which property would you take me to?"

"Hm. Perhaps the one in the Riviera."

"The French Riviera?"

"Sure. Why not?"

"Well, what's stopping us now! Turn the car around!"

Nonetheless, they continued their approach to the house.

"I think it's time I retire for the evening," Alton said, pulling the car into the garage.

She slid out and opened the door for Armmie. At the end of the hallway where their rooms split off, Armmie and Alton looked at each other for a long moment, as if each was burning to say something. Alton held her in her gaze, studying. That little crease between her furrowed brows just about made Armmie's heart collapse. She had never been such a fool in her life.

"So, did you enjoy the show?"

"Isn't it bedtime?" Alton asked.

"You could stand to stay up a few more moments." Alton checked her watch.

"It's late. I'll report to you in the morning."

"You will not melt if you're awake for ten more minutes, Alton," Armmie said.

"And what are you to do if I fall asleep standing up? I'm much too heavy for you to carry."

"One, you underestimate me. And two, I'll just bring you a blanket till morning."

"You couldn't carry me."

"I'm certain I could."

"I don't believe it for a second," Alton said.

Armmie didn't need more than that. She marched over to Alton and scooped her up in her arms. She was admittedly heavier than Armmie had initially prepared for; at this point, she was so determined to lift Alton that sheer willpower kept Alton grasped in her arms. Armmie deposited her at her door.

"Color me impressed," Alton said.

"Did you enjoy the show?"

"I thought it was good. Not my favorite."

"Is that why you cried?"

"Oh, that's what this is about?"

"I'm just curious now what you would do if the show were your favorite."

"I'd probably throw myself from the balcony screaming and naked," Alton said dryly.

"I'd pay to see that," Armmie replied.

"To see me screaming or naked?"

"Can't it be both?"

Alton raised an eyebrow.

"Goodnight, Ms. Charon."

And then she went into her room and shut the door, the devil.

"*Plasticine Dolls* was an interesting one to me. I felt that the concept of entombment evidently plagued the protagonist, informing her obsession with seeing her peers as manipulable for her own enjoyment. Truly a fascinating read," Armmie said, handing the report to Alton.

"Interesting indeed."

"What did you think of it?"

"I found it rather droll. Yes, the protagonist viewed her fellows as toys for her own enjoyment, but it stemmed from a place of unfathomable insecurity. Why do you think I say this?"

"Is this some kind of quiz?"

"Perhaps."

"Are you going to affect my scores?"

"I haven't decided yet."

"Oh, please."

"All right, since you insist. Yes, I will affect your scores."

"Alton!"

"Armmie. What was the moment?"

Armmie thought for a second. Was it when the protagonist spied on her classmates in the locker room? Was it when she fought with her boyfriend about his wandering eyes?

"The fountain?"

"What about the fountain?"

"When she spoke to the police captain."

"What makes you think that?"

"Well, she seemed to talk about the supposed killer in the third person. And the way she described the supposed killer, there was a sense of enamoration, as though she wished she could be the killer. As if she envied the killer because she couldn't stand herself. She wishes to detach herself and become someone else entirely, even if it means projecting herself onto a maniac."

"Hm. Well done. You've passed."

Alton put down her clipboard.

"What do you write? While I'm speaking?"

"I take notes of what I agree with and disagree with."

"You are unbelievable."

"Why is that?"

"Because even when you aren't doing work, you're making yourself work more. Don't you ever relax?"

"I am relaxed."

"You may be the least relaxed person I have ever met in my life."

"Then you ought to meet more people."

"I fancy a drink," Armmie said.

"I hope you enjoy one."

"And you'll join me, I presume?"

"Why would you presume such a thing?"

"Because it's something a relaxed person would do."

Alton rolled her eyes.

"I find you confounding."

"I find you right in front of me."

"Fine. One drink."

"Yes. And I apologize for absolutely torturing you. I'm sure the worst pain you've ever felt in your life is when you're with me."

"I certainly would not say that."

"Wow. That was almost a compliment."

"So, shall I fix you one?"

"I do declare."

Alton grinned.

"My parents acquired an extensive collection of wines before they died. Perhaps we can enjoy the fruits of their labor."

That's how they found themselves sipping a bottle of red in the kitchen. Then two bottles. Then two and a half bottles. Then they finished that bottle.

"Oh, I'm feeling it now," mumbled Armmie.

"Who...who finished all that wine?"

"I think it was us, Alty."

"Ah. Oops."

"Leave bottle. Go to bed."

"Mm-hmm."

On the stairs, Armmie had a realization.

"Alty, I've never seen your room."

"Do you wanna?"

"Yes."

Alton giggled.

"Okay, okay."

They turned the opposite way, holding onto each other for dear life as they clomped down the hall.

"So glad nobody else lives here."

"So GLAD!"

Alton stopped at her door and opened it.

Inside the room was emerald green wallpaper and a four-poster canopy bedframe. The duvet was a complementary shade of green with black details, and the carpet was black. It was unusual, but very elegant.

"Whoa."

"Yup."

"Alton."

"Yes, Armie."

"Help me get my dress off."

"I... shouldn't."

"Then I'll be in it all night."

Alton studied her for a drunken moment, the gears turning. For a quizzical second, Armmie thought maybe Alton would say no. But she stepped toward Armmie and held her in place with one hand and then used the other to reach the top of Armmie's dress. Her fingers fumbled before clasping the zipper and tugging it tortuously down Armmie's back.

When it split open, Alton put her hands on Armmie's hips, faced her away, and then watched fiendishly as the dress momentarily stretched over the mound of Armmie's hips, then fell, inch by inch, down her legs. She turned to face the fully clothed Alton, who chewed on her lip in restraint. Armmie held Alton at arm's length by the shoulders. She looked at her shirt.

"I want this off."

"Huh?" Alton hiccuped.

Armmie slid her hand down Alton's shirt to the first button. Through hazy concentration, Armmie fiddled it open. Then the next, then the next. Alton stared at her, saying nothing, but doing nothing to stop it. Then the final button. Her shirt opened. Armmie untucked it from Alton's pants and tore it off. She sank to her knees, undid Alton's belt, and slid that off too. She slowly, so slowly, undid the buttons on Alton's trousers. Armmie put her hands on Alton's hips, tugging them down to reveal a black, lacy pair of underwear. A faint gasp tumbled from Alton as Armmie pressed her lips against Alton's inner thigh and bit her gently.

She turned around to face the now scantily clothed Alton, who was surveying both choices of Armmie's undergarments. Neither of them said a word. They just stared, breath ragged. Alton put a hand on Armmie's stomach, and Armmie moaned aloud. She wanted to feel shame, but all she felt was aching. For more.

She placed her hand on Alton's back, tugging her in, so that they stood face-to-face. Heads knocked, each ran hands up and down the other's body, as if to carve the other out of clay. Alton ran her hand along the line of Armmie's brassiere, stopping at the clasp.

"We shouldn't," murmured Armmie in Alton's ear, despite everything she actually felt. That her body wanted Alton's fingers to complete their task of opening her brassiere, to hold what was underneath. In fact, she wanted even more than that.

Alton removed her fingers from Armmie's ribcage and instead slipped Armmie's earlobe into her mouth, dragging it through her teeth. She put her hands in Armmie's hair and pulled gently from the base, rolling Armmie's head back. Alton hovered her mouth above

Armmie's tilted neck, her breath causing Armmie's skin to prickle. Armmie moved closer, her body pressing against Alton's. They stilled. Alton's heart beat into Armmie.

Wordless and entranced, they moved to the bed. On impact, they both seemed to remember where they were and what they were doing. Alton looked at Armmie. Armmie returned the gaze. She closed her eyes and fell asleep.

Chapter Five

Armmie finished her report on *The Broken Phonograph*, approved by Alton. Then they began on the classics—formative texts to literature, which Armmie deemed boring and antiquated. She felt the characters were unrelatable to the modern day, though she could draw a few parallels between early works and what authors these days were utilizing, she supposed. Perhaps she could understand why Alton had instructed her to read books like *A Few Copper Coins* and *The Adventures of Tim Turner*. But that didn't make them any less dreary. She was not a fan of this unit in the slightest. However, by this point in the year, the days were growing longer. The sun poked through the clouds more and more. The weather wasn't so abysmal.

Armmie read by lamplight outside one evening, *Sunset in Rome*, when she noticed Alton in her periphery.

"Alton?"

"Yes?"

"Why do you have me reading this book?"

"What do you mean?"

"I fail to see how *Sunset in Rome* is going to improve my overall education."

"Do you find it displeasing?"

"No. But I don't feel I'm learning anything."

"Then you aren't paying enough attention."

The book in question? A romance. Between vampires. Italian vampires. He, a gentle, feminine male, and she, a masculine female. It was quite silly.

"Why are you having me read it?"

"You'll have to tell me during your report."

Oh, blast it. Alton was so slippery when it came to answering a question with a straight answer.

"Listen to this: 'Lover, for it is you that my day rises. Though I cannot see the sun, the rays of your smile shall warm my undead heart.'"

"What is the issue?"

"It just seems out of character for you to recommend me a book such as this. Have you read it?"

"I have."

"That's a shock."

"Now, why is that?"

"Because I presumed you only read macabre books of morals and wisdom."

"I don't know why you would think such a thing."

"You are stern. And uninterested in the frilly." Armmie held up the book. "Which is exactly what this is."

"Perhaps you do not know me as well as you
believe."

"Perhaps you do not let me."

Alton raised an eyebrow. Then she held out a
cigarette and a match.

Armmie scooted over. The sun had set now, and the
stars twinkled in the inky night sky. Alton lit the
cigarette, and fire bloomed at the end. A cloud of
smoke drifted from Alton's lips and into the air. She
handed it to Armmie, who took it in her own lips and
puffed.

"I found the maroon doors," Armmie said, studying
Alton's face. Immediately, a wave of cold seized Alton.

It was true. Armmie had been exploring in what
she would argue is well within her right to do, given
her stay, when she found them at the end of an
obscure hall. This wing had clearly fallen into
disrepair. Alton dusted nothing. The credenzas, the
chairs, the lamps, everything had a thick layer of gray.
Alton clearly walked right past it. But the maroon
door's gold handles showed almost constant use.
Armmie had put her eye up to the crack, hoping to get
a peek inside, but the room was dark.

"And?" Alton clipped, tension fusing her jaw.

"And I didn't go inside. But you owe me an answer.
What is behind the doors?"

"Why must you insist on knowing everything?"

"I have an inquisitive mind."

Alton snorted.

"I can't tell you."

"Why do you have a pile of bodies? All of your applicants' past? Hordes of money? Stolen jewels? Probably, if I could guess."

Alton didn't move. Armmie took a drag of the cigarette and handed it to Alton as smoke billowed from her mouth.

"Fine. If you will not tell me, at least tell me why you can't tell me."

With a pensive look, Alton put the cigarette to her lips. Breathed in. Breathed out.

"I can't fathom any other way to be. No one has ever wanted to know me."

"Who said I want to know you? I just want to know what's behind those doors."

Alton sighed.

"I can't tell you because I don't know how you'll react. I don't want you to change how you look at me."

"But do you think Leandro could ever love Francessca if he never left his crypt?"

Alton chuckled.

"I don't need you to love me..."

Armmie smiled with tight lips and swallowed the knot in her throat.

"...but I do need you to respect me," Alton finished.

"You don't know how I'm going to respond."

"That's precisely the problem."

Armmie took the cigarette from Alton's hand. She tried to suck down the gnawing sadness with the smoke. Gray, unfurling clouds wafted to the heavens in plumes of burnt smoke.

"Why did you choose me?"

"Choose you?"

"For the scholarship. Surely you had thousands of applicants."

"There were a few," Alton mused.

"Why me?"

Alton took the final embers of the cigarette to her beautiful, luscious lips that—

"Because you seemed lonely."

"Oh gee. Thanks."

"And because I was too."

She ashed the cigarette.

"Was?"

"Goodnight, Armmie."

"Goodnight, Alton."

Then she was gone. Her absence created a hole that was not there before she arrived. To think, Armmie was sitting out here, enjoying her evening and her Italian Vampires, and then Alton came, disturbed her, and she was much worse off now that Alton had gone. Armmie had half a mind to call after her. To accuse her of witchcraft or something of the like. Lonely? Armmie wasn't lonely. She was alone. Sure, she didn't have anyone. Well, she had Mel. When she was a child. And her neighbors, Mr. Crag and Mrs. Crag.

Alton misunderstood her. Projected upon her. She was fine before she met Alton. Yes, she was alone... but Armmie was only lonely when Alton left.

Armmie had been munching on a Mrs. Welshire's original chocolate cookie when she accidentally—it was accidentally—bumped into Alton in a dimly lit corridor.

"Are you retiring for the evening?" Armmie asked.

"I am."

"I wish I could remember what your bedroom looks like. I fear I was not in my right mind last time I was there."

"Nor was I."

"It seems unfair that you know my room intimately, but I can't recall where it is you hole up for your evenings."

"Why do you need to know that?"

"You are so Leandro."

"Perhaps it was a mistake for me to suggest that book," Alton furrowed her brow.

"Suggest? Suggest!" Armmie scoffed. "Alton, everything you do is a demand."

Alton chuckled.

"Goodnight, Armmie."

Armmie watched as Alton walked down the dim hall. She watched the swing of her hips, the hang of her hands. Her impossibly straight posture. Alton became a silhouette as she reached the end of the hallway.

"Are you watching me?" Alton asked, not turning around.

"No."

Alton turned. For some inexplicable reason, her heart thundered. Her chest tightened. Then Alton walked down the hall, back to where Armmie stood, planted. Her steps were slow and measured. She reached Armmie after a few moments that felt like a lifetime, as though a magnet inside her was pulling at the opposite magnet in Alton's chest. She reached Armmie and looked down at her.

"Is there something you want to say?" Alton murmured.

The smoothness of her voice, the quiet trouble in her tone... Armmie's pulse picked up. She watched as Alton lifted her hand and caressed Armmie's cheek. Then again, by her lips. She leaned in, holding Armmie's jaw steady, and licked the corner of Armmie's mouth. Armmie sucked in a breath and looked at Alton incredulously.

"You had chocolate on your face," she whispered, and then was gone.

Armmie lay in bed in a nightgown. Once again, consciousness plagued her. By Alton's soft, warm tongue. Her infuriating... everything. She sincerely could not believe the grasp this woman had on her. And furthermore, the grasping she wished Alton would do to her. It was not that Armmie had ever truly been determined to be chaste or save herself for some faceless man. As far as she was concerned, she had no doting mother to soothe and no overbearing father to appease. Love would come in time. Her little cat. Why shouldn't it be Alton? Here was that infernal voice once more, demanding answers to questions Armmie had no interest in entertaining. Alton was from a different world. Alton measured and disciplined. And she was not emotionally available.

She had made it abundantly clear outside. "I don't need you to love me. I need you to respect me."

Why not both? Oh, blast it. She was incorrigible. They both were, in fairness. Both strong-willed and fierce. Whatever. Armmie turned on the light by her bedside and grabbed *Sunset in Rome.*

The page she was on read something incredibly... queer.

"Leandro slipped his hand beneath the folds of Francessca's dress. Their teeth clashed, and as the sensation grew between the fleshy parts of Francessca's thighs—"

This was too much. Armmie should put this foul book down. How lewd! How positively lewd. Alton wanted her to read this filth? Armmie. Put. The book. Away. Armmie opened the book back up.

"Until the tension within Francessa's mortal bones erupted into a searing wash of pleasure. Leandro bit onto the neck of Francessa as she rode his fingers—"

Rode his fingers? How would she even do that? Armmie imagined Francessca, her long flowing black hair, climbing aboard Leandro's fingers like a cowgirl saddling a horse. How hilarious. Then she imagined Francessca sinking onto Leandro's fingers, how that might feel. And then the motion, the rocking back and forth and bouncing up and down, and how that might feel. What Alton's fingers might feel like as she bobbed—*stop. Stop this at once. Only trouble will come from these thoughts.*

She closed the book. Best she read this after a run or something distracting because a certain feeling had returned. Her right hand better not betray her. Her right hand was now creeping toward that certain area throbbing most unpleasantly, and Armmie did not know what to do about it. Perhaps Leandro would.

She opened the book back up. *No one will know.* Her family was gone. She had no friends to speak of. The only person who even spoke to Armmie was Alton, and Alton was the one who required her to read the damn book. It would be between Armmie and herself.

"She rubbed small circles at the top of her..." Armmie closed her eyes so as not to read that word. So Armmie followed in Francessca's footsteps, so to speak, and rubbed small circles on the top of her... and immediately her eyes shot open. *THAT* was what had been hiding out between her legs this whole time? Oh, it felt good. It felt beyond good. It felt like being bent over by firm hands. Armmie picked up the pace, as Francessca no doubt would do.

"The nerve grew sensitive, the knot within her pelvis tightening. The tips of her toes tingled as the pleasure built. Leandro's motion in synch with her own brought to a shattering clim—"

A guttural moan ripped from Armmie's mouth as she lived Francessca's experience. Why on earth had Alton told her to read this book? After a shocking amount of convulsion, the tension in her body relaxed. What an unusual experience. But she could not fathom why she had been shirking this her whole life. To derive such pleasure from a few hand motions? Fantastic. She set the book down, turned off the lights, and dreamed of fingers.

Alton brought down a fresh stack of four books and placed them on the table.

"Theology unit," Alton said. "I've provided some of my favorite texts on religious beliefs."

"Oh joy," murmured Armmie.

"You will enjoy it, I think."

"Will I ever."

Alton shook her head.

"Do or don't. I expect your reports nonetheless." Alton paused. "Perhaps you will be able to join in the conversation. I'm hosting some scholars at our house this weekend. Friends of mine."

"I didn't know you had friends."

"Well, congratulations, you've learned something new."

"And you're going to let me out of my cage for this?"

"Oh, spare me, Armmie. Have I ever denied you?"

"I'm sure I could come up with an example or two."

"While you think on your mistreatment, perhaps you could help me prepare. It's a kind of summit. We will be presenting our findings on the topic of subjugation of lower classes through subliminal messaging in monotheistic religions."

"What are your findings?"

"You will have to wait along with the rest of the scholars."

"And how many people am I to expect?"

"A few," Alton muttered.

Alton was terser than usual the days leading up to the weekend. Which seemed almost impossible, yet Alton was short in both responses and temperament. Dinners were silent and underwhelming. Alton went on no walks; instead, instead studying texts in solitude. In the sitting room, Alton was elsewhere.

"In conclusion, devout followers of the doctrine found themselves at the mercy of an unanswering deity to their own detriment, and such doctrine overwhelmingly led to disappointment in a life unlived," Armmie finished.

Alton tapped her pen on her notebook.

"Overwhelmingly led to disappointment in a life unlived," Armmie emphasized.

"Alton."

Nothing.

"Alton!" she snapped.

"Yes?" Alton replied.

"I spent the last three days poring over mind-numbing religious texts and writing this report. The least you could do is acknowledge me."

"Well done," Alton said. "You've been acknowledged."

A twinge of sadness tickled Armmie's throat. *Keep your chin up, Armmie.* She handed the report to Alton with a courteous smile and bowed out of the sitting room.

Then, in the hall, she sucked in a deep breath. What was happening? Droplets of water threatened to fall from her eyes. She blinked them back. Allergies. Only allergies. Was this just how it was? Alton's plaything until other people entered the mix, and she was no longer a source of entertainment. She did not have the same level of classical education. She was not so learned as the scholars and as Alton herself, and had never felt it like now. Perhaps it was her fault for thinking she could be anything different.

"Armmie?" Alton called down the hallway.

Armmie turned, half expecting Alton to reach her, to embrace her, to say she was sorry for being so cold. Armmie turned.

"You forgot the date on your report."

Armmie sighed. Where that desire came from was beyond her.

"Forgive my transgression, Ms. Tyner," Armmie said, "I'll fix it right now."

Alton raised a brow. Armmie scribbled the date.

"As you were."

And then Armmie walked off, able to leave Alton standing alone for once.

Every time she would pass Alton scrubbing through page after page of text, furiously scribbling notes, she had to catch herself from approaching. How Alton managed straight posture even when hunched over was beyond Armmie. She looked so beautiful, chewing on her lip, tucking falling strands of hair from her pinned French twist. Armmie wanted her so badly. But she couldn't quite say how she wanted her. She was jealous of the pen Alton wrapped her fingers around, jealous of the pages Alton turned. She was jealous of the teacups she put her lips on and

jealous of the sweets she licked with her tongue. And
all the while, Alton flashed quick, tight smiles at
Armmie, as if to say, *"You understand, don't you?"* But
the problem was Armmie didn't understand. How
could she become so second-rate so easily? What did
a stupid summit have over her?

The scholars arrived by car as the sun set. They
filed in, wearing perfectly tailored suits and jackets,
with hats and coats and pointy shoes. Armmie had to
admit they were a little foreboding. Alton had hired a
sort of catering company from town to help prepare
food and drink for the guests. Alton smiled and waved
and greeted her guests with valor and poise that
Armmie assumed Alton broke out for special
occasions. The mark of an aristocrat, no doubt.
Armmie imagined Alton probably endured countless
hours of debutante training. She could not help but
wonder what exactly led Alton to be that way. Perhaps
because her whole family died under tragic
circumstances.

Those thoughts did not linger long as Alton swept
her into conversations with various academics and
scientists.

"She is my pupil," Alton said, gesturing to a frozen-
in-place Armmie.

"Ah, the recipient of the famous scholarship," said a fat man in a pinstripe suit and cane, "how are you finding it?"

Armmie continued to smile politely until Alton nudged her.

"I'm finding it everywhere in this house."

The man laughed raucously.

"Beautiful and funny," the man said. "I'm John Mathews Cromwell. How do you do?"

"I do it all," Armmie said.

He laughed again.

"Good choice, Tyner. I look forward to chatting with you after the talk!"

Cromwell caned off.

Alton looked at Armmie.

"Perhaps we could rely less on humor and more on grace," Alton murmured to Armmie.

"Of course. Thank you for tightening my strings," Armmie bowed. "I look forward to being your marionette, puppeteer."

Then she stormed off with as much of that requested grace as possible.

Appetizers were passed out, drinks flowed, and Alton ignored her except to shove her into conversation with her peers. Not Armmie's peers, to clarify, but Alton's. Armmie felt small. For once, she was not alone, but she felt lonely. Oh, so lonely.

The crowd was guided into the ballroom, a ballroom Armmie just learned existed, where a makeshift stage had been constructed and a hundred seats laid out.

Alton took to the stage.

"Hello all. As you may very well know, my name is Alton Von Tyner, recipient of the Golden Scholar for my research in the theological, as well as discoveries and decoding of ancient texts."

Light applause came from the room.

"I was presented with a variety of historical literature, and if you'll permit me, I shall share my findings with the rest of the London Learning Society —and thanks all for making the journey."

And then she began her talk, highlighting what she described as clear evidence of early communications between the early Barbitian and Grecopotameian peoples. How they communicated, as their gods seemed the same, how their legends highlighted the same discoveries, their myths spoke to the same folklore. She concluded that there must have been a river that had since dried up between the two civilizations. When she finished, the crowd broke into a standing ovation. Then Cromwell moved up to the stage.

"Alton Von Tyner, you have done it again. It is the LLS's great honor to present you with the Pioneer Award for your landmark accomplishments in the discipline!" Cromwell cheered.

Alton looked truly happy for maybe the first time since Armmie had known her. A pang of something unidentifiable ran through her. Why could she not make Alton that happy? She was just another academic chore to Alton. Was it even worth it? Armmie mulled the thought in her head. Should she go? But she recalled that this scholarship truly wasn't for leisure, as Alton had continuously reminded her. She should have taken that advice to heart. It was her fault for ever getting involved. Alton clearly did not feel the same. She would keep her chin up, get through the scholarship, and go to the University of Prague as she had goddamn intended.

Her face must have told a different story, however, as a young woman in a bubblegum dress approached her.

"Pray tell, why do you look glum on this occasion?" said the young woman.

"Just a touch tired, is all," Armmie lied.

"Ah, have you been studying?" she asked. Well, at least she could be honest about that much.

"Quite tirelessly, in fact."

"Well, what have you learned?"

"It might come across as morbid."

"Good! I live for a bit of the macabre."

"All right then." Armmie chuckled. "I studied the major religious texts: The Enchiridion, The Holy Scripture, and The Grimoire, and I must say, they seem to describe the same philosophies. To hear all religions each pontificate about their rightness made me realize that not only is the doctrine of 'I'm right, and the chosen so heed me and my opinions' perpetuated, but it happens in each book. They have each re-written the same ideas. And the reason that an individual chooses a different version of these same ideas is so that they can cling to something that makes death less terrifying. By making this arbitrary choice, everyone who ascribes differently is wrong. And by their being wrong, then that individual must be right."

The young woman just blinked at her. For a moment, a fear flashed through her. Had she said too much? Was this heresy? Was she just flat-out wrong?

"My word. I've never heard anything like that."

"Truly?"

"Truly. Give me one moment. You stay right here and don't move."

So Armmie didn't. Moments later, the woman returned with two gentlemen in tow.

"Go on then, from the top."

Armmie repeated herself. The men looked her over with a sense short of awe.

"Fascinating. You must write that down." One of the men extended a hand. "Cornelius Crank."

Armmie shook it. The other introduced himself as Reginald Hirshfield, and the woman, Rocketta Taylor.

"I must say I'm very impressed," Rocketta said with a smile.

"Well, Alton provided the texts," Armmie replied.

"That scoundrel," said Reginald, "where is the damn girl?"

Armmie glanced over her shoulder to see Alton in conversation with two others who were chatting to her enthusiastically, and she was watching Armmie.

"I haven't the slightest," Armmie said, "but around, no doubt."

"All right, boys, get lost, I'd like to have a chat with the esteemed..."

"Armmie Charon."

"A pleasure to meet you, Armmie."

The gentlemen did indeed get lost.

"I suppose you've got a better footing about this place than I." Rocketta smiled. "Perhaps a bit of air?"

"The balcony is right this way," replied Armmie.

They exited the din of conversation and music to the cool night air.

"I do love this time of year, don't you?" Rocketta said with a pleasant smile.

"I'm inclined to agree."

"Have you enjoyed your scholarship with Tyner thus far? Or are you coming to such conclusions of your own accord?"

"On that front, the credit belongs to her. Her collection of literature is seemingly endless, to say the least. Though I don't know where she keeps it all."

"Well, the library, of course."

"There is a library?"

"Sure. It's two floors," Rocketta said, and pointed to a large part of the manor that rose above the rest.

"You've been?"

"Why of course! Her parents used to throw parties there practically every night."

"Pardon my asking, but... Did she change much? After they passed?"

Rocketta looked around.

"Between you and me, darling, that Alton, while quick as a whip, has always been a little... odd. I don't know what happened behind closed doors, frankly, as her siblings seemed to have equally... disturbed dispositions. Though I hate to speak ill of the dead. May they all rest."

Hm. Disturbed was not the word she might use to describe Alton, though perhaps she did not know her at all. She knew a façade, or a prepared version. And in retrospect, Alton had a little bit of a temper.

"Though, Ms. Charon, I do request that we not discuss another," Rocketta said.

"Oh? And why is that?"

"Because I'd like to talk about you. You're quite a dashing lady, if I do say so. I should very much like to get to know you."

"You flatter me, Ms. Taylor." Armmie smiled. "Though I must say I am charmed."

Rocketta was, in truth, very beautiful. Short black hair, smooth, chestnut skin, and rather well endowed... to say the least.

"Have you ever been dancing? In London?"

"I can't say I have."

"Well then, you must come visit! I think you'll find it quite agreeable."

"I have lived in London for most of my life," Armmie said.

"Oh! Then why on earth have I never seen you?"

Namely because she was a poor nobody with no prospects or family that lived in a tiny apartment and wore threadbare hand-me-downs and ate like a peasant.

"I don't get out much."

"Then you and Alton are compatible at least in that regard," she hummed. "Though perhaps a change of pace might suit you."

"What do you have in mind?"

"Myself, of course. Unless that's too forthright, in which case I'll say different scenery."

"My scholarship still has nearly nine and a half months to go."

"I understand, but has the old girl given you a holiday or two?"

"As a matter of fact, she has."

"And I don't suppose you had any plans of going and being with something as boring and trivial as family."

Definitely not.

"None to speak of."

"Well, I'm terribly sorry for your loss and theirs. Though I would just simply love to show you Italy. Have you ever been?"

Definitely not.

"Not yet. But I would love a tour guide."

"Lucky for you, I am part Italian."

"Oh?"

"You can't tell from my golden complexion?"

"I'd have to take a closer look."

Armmie moved closer.

"My, you do have radiant skin."

"None so radiant as your own. And what lovely hair you have," Rocketta said, twirling a lock of Armmie's hair.

They stared over the dark gardens for a time before Rocketta spoke again.

"Have you ever been with a woman?" Rocketta asked.

Yes. No. Maybe? Not in that way. But... yes?

"It's complicated," Armmie replied.

"Ah. Is it complicated or is she complicated?"

"Let us say both."

"Well, darling, if she cannot see what is right in front of her, the genius may not be as smart as she appears."

"You're just saying that."

"Armmie, I don't just say anything. You can ask anyone I've ever spoken to, and I can assure you they will confirm. I know what I like."

"Are you implying you like me?"

"Is it so wrong to say that I do?"

"You hardly know me, Rocketta."

"Oh, but even the way you say my name," she trilled. "Well, don't let me get carried away. But sincerely, Armmie, let me show you what uncomplicated looks like."

She rubbed a gloved hand up Armmie's arm, resting it on her shoulder. She smelled good, Armmie would give her that. Like jasmine and tuberous. Floral and sweet. Not of wood and smoke.

Out of the corner of her eye, Armmie noticed someone on the balcony. Someone, stone-faced, with sleeves rolled up, was watching her every movement.

Armmie turned away, smug.

"I'd best get inside before I make a grand fool of myself." Rocketta grinned.

"Impossible."

They hooked arms and walked back inside.

The party had died down, folks on couches putting their coats on.

Cornelius approached Armmie, Rocketta still linked by the elbow.

"Ms. Charon, I must say you had a fascinating perspective. If you should ever like to meet with the London Learning Society, please take my card. It includes all modes of my correspondence." He shook her hand enthusiastically.

"We are staying in town at The Pauper's Inn until the morning, if you would join us for a breakfast of sorts." Rocketta smiled. She curtsied and kissed the top of Armmie's hand before walking out with Cornelius.

She turned over her shoulder just as John Mathews Cromwell (did he use all three names?) put on his bowler hat.

"You kids be good now," Cromwell said through a throaty chuckle.

"Will we ever," Alton said with a placid smile.

The last of the caterers filed out the door, bidding their farewells.

Then it was just Armmie and Alton. Alton, who was boring holes into Armmie's skull with her eyes.

"Congratulations on your honor, pioneer."

"Congratulations on your newfound friends. That Rocketta is a dear, isn't she?"

Something in Alton's tone was ruthless. And insincere, to say the least.

"If you don't like her, why did you invite her?"

"I never said I didn't like her. I am curious what you left the party to chat about."

"She invited me to Italy during my holiday."

Silence. Then...

"Did she now?" Alton clenched her jaw. "She has been known to throw out an invitation to any warm body who will look twice in her direction."

"Oh, so you think that the only reason someone might look at me with interest is if they were a floozie? I'm only worth a call girl?"

"That's not what I meant."

"Well, it's what you said."

"Armmie, don't deliberately misinterpret what I'm saying."

"I'm not misinterpreting anything."

Pause. Alton crossed her arms.

"I wouldn't trust her."

"And why should I trust what you think? You've hardly been forthcoming or even honest. I mean, for the love of it, Alton, I don't even know you."

"You don't know me?"

"Do I? I mean, all I know is that your family is buried in the cemetery and you're rich. And you like to read."

"If that's all you've been able to surmise, then I've severely overestimated you."

Armmie stepped back.

How could she respond to that? Tears pricked in her eyes once more. *Hold them in Armmie, just a few more moments.* One fell, then another. She turned from Alton and walked away.

She made it to her room and closed the door, barely making it in before collapsing to the floor, tears now streaming down her face. Armmie pulled her knees to her chest and rested her throbbing head against them. She wanted to go. Few things had ever hurt this badly. The cat had been so close she could almost pet it. What had she done to scare it off? Or had it ever really been there in the first place? Was it so unreasonable that someone could love her? Strangely enough, Armmie never truly understood how she felt about Alton until now. Armmie rocked back and forth, crying to herself.

A faint knock on the door. Armmie stood, doing her best to wipe her face.

"It's open."

The door swung open. There stood Alton, holding a tray with a cookie and two teacups. She had been muscling herself up for this, that much was clear. Her gaze softened as she beheld a tearful Armmie.

"Armmie," she breathed.

Armmie just sniffled.

"I brought you these," Alton said.

"Okay."

"Can I come in?"

"All right," Armmie mumbled.

Alton came in and set the tray on the coffee table, but didn't sit.

"I'm sorry I made you cry."

Oh no. Here come the tears again.

Armmie did her best to wipe her face with the sleeves of her dress.

"I didn't mean what I said."

"That's not why I'm upset, Alton."

She put her hands in her pockets.

"Well then, what is it?"

"Do you truly not know?"

"I mean, perhaps I was busy this week."

"Busy? I could barely get a word in between all your silence. Do you just not care about me at all? Am I less important to you than your reading?"

"My reading is very important."

"Then what are you doing here?"

"Because I don't wish to upset you."

Wrong answer.

"The correct answer was, 'but you're more important,'" Armmie said, throat tight. Alton stared at her.

"Can't they both be important?"

They could. But one was human, and the other was a stack of books. Armmie was wrong for thinking Alton felt differently.

"What's behind the maroon doors?"

Alton's eyes widened. There was an unmistakable fear there. Armmie almost felt bad for pushing. Couldn't she wait until Alton was ready? But whenever would that be? The words seemed to dance on Alton's tongue, prying to get out. But her jaw remained shut. Armmie was not getting an answer tonight.

"Goodnight, Alton."

Armmie moved to shut the door and closed it gently. But she heard no footsteps leave. She heard a faint thunk, like someone putting their forehead on the door. Armmie wished for Alton to throw open the door, to tell her what was so horrible she was hiding because Armmie didn't care. She didn't care what Alton hid, whatever skeletons, evidence, or proof of evil Alton was hiding. She wanted Alton. All of Alton. But Alton would not give it to her. And how long could Armmie wait before she admitted to herself that the version of Alton she hoped for would never come?

She waited and waited for footsteps to go, but they didn't. Eventually, Armmie understood Alton would not open the door. So Armmie picked herself off the floor and crawled into bed while the tea got cold and the cookies went uneaten.

Chapter Six

In the morning, Armmie arrived downstairs to a breakfast table full of food. Griddlecakes, eggs, sausage, orange juice, fruit, coffee, scones.

Armmie was a little aghast. All this food?

Alton walked in wearing gray linen pants and a matching gray linen vest. She looked quite... quite good.

"Who is all this food for?"

"For us." Alton smiled.

Damn. Oh, damn.

"Alton... I sent for a taxi to take me to town. Many of the scholars are at The Pauper's Inn, and I was going to join them for breakfast."

Crestfallen. Armmie had never known it before until now.

"But you should come. I'll help you put this away, and you can join me."

"There's no need. Enjoy your new friends."

She seemed sincere, yet... downtrodden. Really, truly crestfallen.

Armmie was still carrying the sadness she felt about Alton to the inn, where Reginald, Cornelius, and Rocketta all sat at the end of a long table of last night's festivities' patrons. They were chatting about wayward philosophies, next week's parties, and the contents of Alton's talk.

Rocketta stood and greeted her with a brief hug. To be pressed upon her bosom was.. Well...

"I am so glad you could join us." Rocketta grinned. "Have you brought Alton?"

"I'm afraid not. She was spent after such a late night."

"But of course," Rocketta said, "though I cannot say I am too upset by her absence at this very moment."

"Don't flirt with me before breakfast," Armmie quipped.

She thought about Alton at the breakfast table. All that food. She must have spent hours preparing it. And Armmie had left her. She shouldn't have come. She should have stayed.

"So, Armmie, what books are next for you?" Reginald asked.

"Well, I haven't received my next four assignments yet, but I believe in philosophy."

"I'm excited by the prospect of hearing your opinions," Cornelius said.

"You flatter me," Armmie said.

"Perhaps you should publish your works? My dear friend Jasper runs a newspaper. You've heard of the *Daily Inquirer*?"

Armmie choked on her drink. Oh, she had heard of it.

"Armmie darling, are you all right?"

"Quite. What a wonderful opportunity, but… Who would want to read my silly two-page essays?"

"Why, anyone with a spare few minutes," Reginald said.

"Jasper! Jasper!" Cornelius snapped his fingers. The man named Jasper, a fellow in a three-piece suit, sat at the table.

"What am I, the help?" Jasper joked. "Go on and spit it out."

The help.

"We'd like to propose to you a new section in the paper. Excerpts from the reviews Ms. Charon here has written." Rocketta smiled gracefully.

"Oh?" Jasper asked.

"I think you'll find them quite entertaining. She is a wonderful writer," Rocketta said, leaning in. "You are a good writer, aren't you?"

"Yes," Armmie whispered back.

"A great writer, in fact," Rocketta reaffirmed.

"I shall have to check with the rest of the board, but send me some copies of your work. We may be able to run it," Jasper said, extending a hand. "Jasper Bonaparte."

"Armmie Charon."

She shook. He nodded politely and headed back to his seat.

"Rocketta! You did not need to do such a thing," Armmie said.

"You can thank me later, darling. In fact, I'm feeling daring."

Rocketta handed her a piece of paper with a scribbled address.

"Give me an hour's notice. You can come any time."

An hour is how long it took by car to get back to London.

Armmie folded up the paper, slipping it into the pocket of her cardigan.

The rest of the meal, with light and sweet conversation, flowed as naturally as possible. Though sometimes, Alton's friends were a bit out of touch, saying things like 'there has been dissent at the factory,' and the 'stupid git keeping my yacht hasn't finished cleaning it since last season.' What Armmie truly, truly wanted was Alton. For Alton to be sitting there with a slight smugness, a lilting eyebrow raise, with those hands folded in her lap. But Rocketta was quite charming. She touched Armmie's arms in just the right way, complimenting and nudging her so effortlessly.

Then it was time for them all to pack up their caravan and have a chauffeur drive them back to London. Armmie said her farewells.

"Armmie, I expect you'll send me your work," Jasper said, kissing her cheek in farewell. "Then perhaps you can come to London, and we can discuss it."

"I will mail it to you promptly."

Rocketta squeezed Armmie's hand in goodbye as Phillip pulled the car around. Then she planted a soft kiss, a genuine kiss, on Armmie's temple. Then a second on her cheek. It got something moving downstairs. A slight twinge of something. Rocketta seemed to know it.

"Any time," she promised with a wink.

Armmie got back in the car.

Armmie opened the door to the manor to find it hauntingly empty.

"Alton?" she called through the hallways. "Alton?"

Eventually, she found her in the gardens, in white cropped shorts and a matching shirt, with a cerulean sweater tied around her shoulders.

"Alton?" Armmie said.

"Armmie," Alton said.

"I'm terribly sorry I left before breakfast."

"It's quite all right," Alton said, a little stiff. "You're not bound here."

"Well, something quite excellent happened," Armmie said.

"Oh?"

"You're aware of Jasper Bonaparte?"

"Yes. The fellow's a little out of touch."

"I thought the very same. Anyway, he is offering to publish my reports in the *Daily Inquirer*," Armmie said, attempting to tamp down the squeal in her voice.

Alton looked her up and down.

"Well, that is quite excellent," Alton said, a hint of a smile on her lips. "You'll certainly have no shortage of content."

"You're not mad?"

"Why would I be mad?"

"Because… I don't know if this scholarship is supposed to be private or whatnot."

"A woman's best asset is her freedom," Alton commented. "Furthermore, as mentioned at the party, you seem to be some kind of savant. Why not share your wisdom with the world?"

"Can I tell you something you cannot repeat?"

"Of course."

"I used to work at the *Daily Inquirer*. I quit to come here," Armmie admitted.

"Really?"

"Really. My boss wrote that I was a lousy copy editor and that I would never amount to anything. I hope he doesn't recognize my name."

"Let us not worry. Jasper is an old friend and will make good on his promises."

"Well then. I suppose I am to send my manuscripts to Jasper in the coming weeks."

"I'll have Phillip take it to the post tomorrow."

Alton looked quite... Inexplicable. So effortless. Reserved. Suave.

"Alton..."

"Armmie, I think we should remain cordial in our arrangement," Alton said. "It seems feelings getting in the way will only continue to hinder our academic processes."

Ah. Here we go. Hadn't Alton already said this before? How long did that last?

"As you wish, Alton."

And there was that look. The look that said *fight me. Make me change my mind. I'm lying. This isn't what I want.* But Alton was impossible to reason with. Armmie would move on. She couldn't waste any more time on someone who didn't want her back.

"Are you prepared for your report this evening?"

Oh. Oh no.

"On second thought, I think I must head back to the house immediately."

Lest she like a taste of Alton's ruler. Which—no.

Alton tapped her pen along her notepad thoughtfully.

"And you mean to assert that this communion with nature is actually ancestral knowledge passed to future generations?" Alton asked.

"Well, I'm not saying I believe it; I'm just saying that's what Niet says in this book."

"That's a fair conclusion." Alton put her pen down. "What did you think of it?"

"It was an interesting non-Western perspective on the mysteries of the universe. I'm inclined to think either everyone's got it wrong or everyone's a little right," Armmie said.

A fire crackled in the background. The sun was setting later and later each day, but the night still had a considerable chill.

"What do you think about the matter?" Armmie asked.

"I suppose that none of this matters. And we are very lucky to be where we are," she said, resounding. "I have been studying ancient civilizations for years—their histories, myths, and religions. I must say, they all die. Whether their predictions come true ultimately seems irrelevant when you consider these consensuses change so rapidly between cultures and times that they have no basis anymore. And in our era, I'm not compelled by anything. Which leads me to believe that there is nothing out there for us meager beings."

"Do you think we ought to enjoy ourselves?"

"Surely."

"And not deny ourselves?" Armmie tested.

"I suppose."

Then Alton fell silent, as if contemplating the implications of what Armmie was asking. She was truly not naive enough to think that Armmie was merely curious.

"How did you find dinner?"

Subject change.

"I found it in the kitchen."

"Ha. Funnier every time," Alton said with a slight smile. She wore cotton loungewear, a coordinating set which was chic despite its simplicity.

"It was excellent, Chef," Armmie said, "I've just about forgotten how to cook with you always taking the lead."

"Perhaps I am a tad controlling," Alton muttered.

"Oh no, what makes you say that?"

A hint of a smirk appeared.

"You've done excellent work, Ms. Charon. I'm very pleased with your progress, and I have no doubt that when Jasper receives the first of your manuscripts, he will feel the same."

"You're too kind, Ms. Tyner."

They looked at each other for a moment, Alton studying her with those hazel eyes, with that straight nose and soft lips.

"Shall we dance?"

"Dance? Dance what? And to what music?" Alton asked.

"I'll hum a tune," Armmie said.

"That's unnecessary," Alton replied.

"Nothing is necessary. You said it yourself. If nothing matters, shouldn't we do what we want?"

"And you would like to dance."

"I would."

"And what if I wouldn't like to?"

Armmie frowned.

"Then you can go to bed. Though it's only 8 p.m."

"Young lady, what are you getting at?"

"Nothing, old lady. Just something to do."

Alton crossed her arms.

Armmie hummed a tune her mother used to sing when she was a child. The lyrics were hazy, like the face of the woman who sang them.

Where has my lover gone? Lost to the sea? Just when I found him my lover left me.

It was strange to think that her life had led to this. The apathy of her family had brought her here.

"Come, Alton," Armmie commanded as best she could, "don't let your life pass you by."

Alton rolled her eyes and stood. They swayed and rocked, a little awkwardly, until Alton cracked a smile. She sped her dancing as she hummed her own tune. Armmie recognized it as a song from *Walkin' Atlantic.* They hummed it together in a strange sway. Armmie stepped closer. Alton didn't move. Armmie stepped again. Alton didn't move. Where was this "moving on" Armmie said she would do?

"What are you doing, Ms. Charon?" Alton murmured.

"Nothing that a review board would find inappropriate," Armmie murmured in return.

She clasped Alton's hands and pulled her in, putting her arms on her shoulders. Armmie wrapped her arms around Alton's waist, and they swayed.

"Ms. Charon," Alton warned, not pulling away, "why do you refuse to follow the rules?"

"I will accept the consequences tomorrow."

"I trust you will."

Alton kept her humming. They rocked back and forth until the fire died down. Eventually, Alton excused herself to bed, leaving Armmie alone in the sitting room, enveloped in wood and smoke.

Armmie busied herself with work, now trying to actually make her presentations good, seeing as Jasper Bonaparte would read them. And putting in a little work might be good for her, especially if she might actually go to university at the end of all this. Not might. She was. She would be.

She and Alton had gone for a walk through the garden. It drove her mad because Alton seemed to intentionally be moving her hand out of the way every time they almost brushed. Armmie saw a flower she quite loved. It was bright fuchsia, which was arguably very unusual.

"What kind of flower is this?" Armmie asked.

"This is a filotopis rinarus," Alton replied, "they are known for their honey-like smell."

Armmie leaned in to sniff it. It smelled terrible.

"Ew, this one must be rotted. It reeks," Armmie said, then she saw the impish grin on Alton's face. "Oh, you liar!"

"Apologies," Alton said, putting her hands behind her back.

She was so effortless these days, especially when she pretended like she didn't give a damn about Armmie. Perhaps Alton thought she was being slick with the sidelong glances or her soft staring at mealtimes. Armmie knew better, though.

"I was particularly taken with your interpretation of *Gliding Used*," Alton said. They were making their way back to the house.

"What about it?"

"I liked what you said about the protagonist."

"Remind me?"

"Shouldn't you be reminding me? You just did a presentation on it."

"Yet you're the one who brought it up. It's your interpretation now."

Alton chuckled.

"You suggested the protagonist uses the broken hang glider because she believes in its power to carry her safely to the ground. But why do you think she doesn't care about it? She knows it's been damaged."

It seemed Alton might be talking about something else. Armmie was no detective, but context clues seemed to be important, especially seeing as Alton was attempting to look everywhere but Armmie's eyes.

"I think the protagonist knows the hang glider has a vested interest in getting them both safely to the ground, despite what the hang glider may think about itself."

"So you're suggesting that someone shouldn't care that the thing for which they risk their life could be unfixable?"

"I think the hang glider is reading too much into a silly book."

Alton looked at the ground.

"But... I also think," Armmie continued, "that the protagonist likes her hang glider the way it is."

...

Books piled high, arms completely full, Armmie was trying to make it down the stairs in one trip. She had several books to return to Alton, along with a few items of laundry that needed attending to. It was nice to not have a group of people waiting on her hand and foot, watching her every movement. However, there was a small part of her that *at first* was excited at the prospect of having someone do her wash. It was the thing she envied most about rich people, seeing as folding her own clothes really showed her the true meaning of the word chore.

Alton had warned her on numerous occasions not to walk down the stairs without being able to see her feet, but Alton was paranoid and overly cautious. However, despite having walked up and down these stairs in this exact circumstance countless times before, Armmie's foot missed a step and she tumbled. The rolling down the stairs was not quite so horrible, but the humiliation certainly was. She landed at the bottom with a miserable thud. And she realized her leg *really* hurt.

Alton rushed in.

"Armmie? Are you alright?" There was a sense of urgency in her voice, a genuine concern. If Armmie didn't know any better, she might think Alton liked her.

"Oh, yes." Armmie cleared her throat. "Nothing to see here."

Alton frowned and started clearing up the mess.

"I've told you a thousand times not to do that," she chastised.

"Well, you were right; I was wrong. Is that what you want to hear?"

"Absolutely," Alton replied.

She organized all the books and clothes into a little pile for Armmie to grab. Armmie tried to stand and found it quite painful and also not really possible. She winced and favored her left foot.

"Damn," she hissed.

"Are you alright?" Alton stepped to her. She took some of Armmie's weight off. They walked Armmie to the nearest couch, her doing a fair amount of limping.

Armmie sat, and Alton raised her foot on a pillow.

"It's quite swollen," Alton noticed.

She was astute in her observations. Armmie's whole ankle had blown up. Alton returned with some ice, gently wrapping Armmie's foot in a towel. The pain was bad, but the doting Armmie couldn't help not minding so much. Over the course of the next few days, the doting remained consistent, in fact. Armmie could get used to this. Alton helped her around, carried her things, clucked her tongue at Armmie's hissing. She brought Armmie tea and her meals, fluffed her pillows and blankets.

"I should sprain my ankle all the time," Armmie thought.

"Alton?" Armmie asked. Alton sat beside her on a chaise lounge. Armmie felt positively Victorian, lying weakly, waiting to be serviced. The dramatics were a careful line to walk, though, so as not to show her hand. Her ankle did hurt, to be fair.

"Yes?" Alton asked, looking up from her book. How novel.

"Would you mind terribly massaging my ankle?"

"Of course not."

Now, that was a surprise. Alton set her book down and pressed gently on Armmie's tender foot. Her fingers worked up and around Armmie's foot and ankle, the prolonged touch feeling quite marvelous. Yes, she could get used to this.

Alton made it up to Armmie's calf when Armmie said, "You know, my thigh is quite sore too."

A flicker of recognition shone in Alton's eyes, but she didn't stop. It seemed, on some level, Alton wanted to touch Armmie's thigh.

"That's odd," Alton mused, "you didn't fall on your thigh."

"It's all connected, I'm sure."

Alton worked her way up past Armmie's knee. It was a wonderful combination of squeezing, rubbing, and working Alton's palm in that had Armmie gripping the cushion of the couch. She hit a spot that elicited a certain groan-like sound from Armmie, a little more provocative than just a regular exhale.

"My this must be really helping," Alton murmured.

"It is," Armmie gasped as Alton's delicate touch worked its way far past her mid-thigh. The throbbing sensation in her ankle had moved to a different part of her body entirely. Alton didn't look up at her, but her fingers kept coming closer and closer to the hem of Armmie's skirt.

"Does it hurt up here?" Alton asked, running her hand up Armmie's hip bone. Armmie nodded.

"Mhm."

"And what about here?" Alton had moved to a gentler touch, grazing along her pelvis.

"It's very sensitive," Armmie gasped as Alton's hands trailed lower and lower. The burning, throbbing, pounding, nagging, desperate need started peaking. Armmie moved her hips into Alton's hand, shuddering as those fingers brushed her inner thighs.

Alton looked at Armmie. Armmie looked at Alton. Her fingers were so close to Armmie's underwear, Armmie could exhale and they would be touching. She was afraid to, though, mostly because if she exhaled the moment might end, or she might orgasm on impact.

"It's particularly sensitive between my legs," Armmie whispered.

Alton ran one finger up the front of Armmie's underwear, slowly, deliberately and then pulled her hand away.

"Then I'd best leave it alone."

Armmie wanted to shriek. Alton had such a little smirk on her lips. She knew what she had done, what she was doing. Which was driving Armmie up the wall. If Armmie didn't climax soon, she was going to burst.

There was a shrill ringing noise, one unlike anything Armmie had ever heard. She rushed to Alton. Where was she? Was everything all right?

Armmie found her standing near a window that overlooked the garden, holding a strange contraption.

"Why, she's just come in now," Alton said, "Armmie, it's Jasper."

"Where? I don't see him."

"He's on the phone."

"The phone?"

"Yes. Come here. Put your ear to this and talk as if he is standing beside you."

Alton handed her the C-shaped bit with two cups on either end, which was attached to a cord, and *that* was attached to a box.

"Jasper?"

Through this C, Armmie heard Jasper.

"Yes! Armmie, my dear!" came his voice through the phone, though he was decidedly not in the room.

"Is this a recording of some kind?" Armmie asked, incredulous.

"Jasper, why don't you tell her what you told me?"

"Well, Ms. Charon, I have to say I am absolutely in love with your work. You have a keen wit most modern authors miss," Jasper said. "I'd like to invite you to London to discuss figures and concepts. I won't say more on the phone."

"You couldn't just tell me now?"

"No, no. I insist you come. And bring Tyner. She needs a little fresh air before her retirement," Jasper said.

"When would you like us?" Armmie asked.

"This weekend. Make arrangements," Jasper replied. "I look forward to seeing you both."

Then his voice disappeared.

"Alton, you did not tell me you had this magic machine!"

"It wasn't a secret."

"So you can speak to anyone you'd like?"

"They have to pick up. But yes."

"Fascinating."

"What did the bloke want?"

"He's insisting we come to London."

"I'll arrange for Phillip to take you whenever you desire."

"He explicitly and deliberately insisted that you join me."

"Me? Why?"

"Something about getting you some fresh air before your retirement."

"I'd hardly say London has more fresh air than here." Alton snorted. "I mean, you lived there your whole life. I don't have to tell you."

Armmie couldn't deny that fact.

"Jasper sounded unwavering. I would hate for him to rescind my offer because I didn't follow through on bringing you," Armmie batted her eyes.

"What do you need me for?"

"I don't need you for anything. But evidently, Jasper does. He said this weekend. We will go this weekend. Pack a trunk," Armmie said, once again batting her eyes.

"Oh, fine."

"Wonderful!" Armmie clapped her hands. "We can stay at mine."

"Stay? I thought you meant to go for the day."

"No, no. What if he needs us the following day? Lest we be unprepared."

Alton studied her with crossed arms. Her eyes roved Armmie, picking her apart.

...

That studious look didn't seem to disappear from Alton as they packed their trunks in the car the following Thursday. It was only when Phillip's car pulled into Armmie's crummy neighborhood that she realized that perhaps they should have stayed elsewhere. Any elsewhere. Just short of a tenement, Armmie's apartment was stacked on two others.

"You don't mind a climb, do you?" Armmie asked, a little sheepishly.

"Not at all," Alton said. "I'm looking to get in some exercise before my retirement."

Phillip unloaded the trunks.

"Monday mornin' then?" Phillip asked.

"Yes indeed. Thank you as ever," Alton replied.

Phillip bowed his head, turned over the car, and drove off.

Armmie fiddled with the keys, then they dragged the trunks up the first flight of stairs.

"We can stay somewhere else, you know," Armmie tried.

"That's unnecessary," Alton said.

"You may just find another place a little more comfortable."

"I don't think so."

"It's a little cramped."

"Nonsense."

They cleared the second floor.

"And a little dirty."

"I can manage."

"It may not be up to your standards."

"We are already here, are we not?"

Fair point. They stood outside Armmie's door. It was shabby. Peeling paint, peeling wood. Certainly nothing like Alton had ever seen.

"It's not much better on the inside, I'm afraid."

"Armmie, open the door."

Armmie fumbled with the keys.

"It's just that there is something I forgot to tell you."

"I don't care."

The door creaked open.

"There... there.. is only one bed," Armmie confessed.

This garnered Alton's attention.

"Only one bed?"

"I've never had a guest."

"Well, have you got a couch?"

"I have a chair."

Armmie was immediately thrown back into this tiny place. How small it seemed now. Room one: One window in the kitchen, where the table was, and one lamp. Room two: One bed with a chair and a small desk above it, one lamp. Bathroom in the hall. Armmie struck matches to turn the lamps on.

"I'll sleep in the chair then," Alton said.

"You'll do nothing of the sort."

"You shouldn't sleep in a chair. It's your home."

"You're my guest."

"Then I'll sleep on the floor."

"No, I can sleep on the floor."

"I won't have it."

Armmie put her hands on her hips.

"Alton, you're being difficult."

"I'm being difficult?"

"Just sleep in the bed. I'll sleep on the floor."

"Armmie, you're being difficult."

"Perhaps we should go."

Alton sucked in a breath.

"*The Daily Inquirer*'s office is near?"

"It's a five-minute walk."

"Really?"

"The city gets substantially nicer when you go over the bridge, if that's what you're asking."

"That's not what I meant."

"You're welcome to get a hotel. I invite you to, in fact," Armmie said.

"And how will I get there? Should I send a smoke screen to Phillip?"

"Shall we thumb wrestle for the bed?"

"Your meeting is tomorrow. You need a good night's sleep."

"Oh, blast it, Alton! Just share the bed with me."

Alton blinked.

"Fine."

"Bathroom is down the hall."

"It's not in here?"

"It's in the west wing, if you go past the two-story fountain."

"Hm."

In a flash, Alton was gone. Armmie changed into a threadbare nightgown. Much more threadbare than she realized. It didn't seem so threadbare when she was in her room alone, but when she knew Alton would—

Alton stood in the doorway, once again studying Armmie with her scrutinizing gaze. Of course it was at this very moment that her nipples were on high alert, sticking right out of this gauzy toga of a nightgown. Armmie crossed her arms.

"I'm going to use the restroom," Armmie said quickly.

She heard Alton turn around where she stood as if to watch Armmie's hips sway under the nightgown as she walked down the hall.

When she returned to the room, Alton was sitting on the bed.

"You know how to get under covers, don't you?" Armmie asked.

Alton rolled her eyes and stood, once again, before pulling back the covers.

"After you."

"No, after you."

"Don't you think this arrangement is a bit... queer?" Alton asked.

"It's only queer if you make it."

And she got into bed. Alton stiffly did the same. They faced away from each other, but it didn't make all that much of a difference in truth. Armmie was still pressed against Alton.

How they kept finding themselves in situations such as this was honestly beyond Armmie. Her bed, the one she had slept on practically her whole life, was not empty. In fact, the warmth of wood and smoke filled it. For long moments, Armmie lay awake on her back. She somewhat expected to hear deep breaths, light snoring perhaps. But Alton lay rigid as a board for some reason.

"Stop looking at me," Alton said.

"Don't flatter yourself," Armmie replied, "there's only three directions I could be looking."

Then, nothing.

Alton was at the rigor mortis level of unmoving.

"Alton, why are you being weird?"

"I'm not being weird."

"Have you never shared a bed before?"

A long pause.

"I have."

"With whom?"

"It's none of your business."

"A lover?"

"So what if it was?"

"So nothing. One might think that if you had shared a bed with someone, you would know how to act naturally."

"I am being natural."

"You're naturally like a vampire?"

"Vampires sleep upside down."

"Alton, have you ever been in love before?"

As if Alton could get any stiffer.

"I'd like to use my one question."

"You'd like to know if I've ever been in love? Aren't there any better questions you could ask?"

"I think it's a fairly good question."

"Don't you think you could go a little deeper? Without—"

"Fine, you want me to go deeper? I will." Armmie rolled over to look at Alton, who still had her back turned. "What was your family like behind closed doors?"

A long, deep exhale. It seems Armmie had struck a nerve. *Good.*

"Depending on the day," Alton said, "some days it was picturesque. All the other families always commended us on our appearance, on how beautiful our family was. But to use your words, behind closed doors…"

Alton sucked in another breath. Armmie gently put her hand on Alton's shoulder.

"My parents would send the servants away. My mother was wicked, and my father was a brute. They would lock us in the cupboards. They would cut our hair at the dinner table. They grew hot peppers in the garden. I think they delighted in being creative. Perhaps the money got to their heads. We were their experiments. My poor darling sister was the first to go. I found her hanging in the stairwell. And my brother grew ill after they made him get into the frozen pond behind our house naked. He didn't last much longer. Then I was alone. Perhaps because of the loss, perhaps because of the tarnished image, or perhaps because all their attention was focused on me... my life until they died was quite... painful."

"Is that why you...?"

"No. I just like seeing you bent over."

Armmie scoffed. A conversation for another time.

"That's quite unimaginable, Alton. Thank you for telling me."

"Well, it's history now. And as a result of their careful actions, nothing ever left a mark. Only the psychological damage lasted, but nothing that anyone in the world could see. Just kids complaining about their parents, to the naked eye."

Armmie scooted forward more and more until she could wrap her arms around the rotated Alton.

"Armmie, this isn't necessary."

"It's only queer if you make it. Now be quiet and go to bed."

Eventually, Alton relaxed in her arms. She could scarcely believe it. She was holding Alton. Armmie stayed awake, silently breathing in the scent of Alton until the deep breaths told Armmie she was asleep.

"Wake up, sugarplum," Alton's voice jolted Armmie from bed.

"Huh? Where are we?"

"Your flat, as you'll recall."

Hm. Armmie had completely forgotten that.

"You're going to be late for the meeting."

Armmie bounced out of bed.

"Am I? Oh, what time is it?"

"You'll be fine. I've woken you up with plenty of time," Alton said, already dressed, "but imagine if I hadn't."

Today, she wore tan linen trousers and a matching cropped linen shirt. These summer months were making Alton even more fashionable.

At the meeting, Alton sat outside Jasper's office. She insisted that she not go in. No, this was all Armmie, she said.

"So, Armmie, my dear, I'm a superfan. Now, obviously, we can't run all two pages of your reports twice a week."

Her heart sank a little. What had she expected? That they were just going to put her on the front page? After she had quit the paper, no less?

"But I believe it will give the readers something to get excited about. I'd like to offer you a column in the Entertainment section. We will run a half-page per issue. I'd like to buy your first five reports as a trial, meaning we will have a ten-week run." Jasper cleared his throat. "After which time, we will evaluate the performance and might purchase more papers to come. What do you think?"

"I think it sounds wonderful," Armmie said, "how much are you looking to buy the papers for?"

Jasper replied. Armmie had to stifle a gasp.

"Sounds like a deal?"

"Deal."

They shook on it.

"You'll send the papers by mail?"

"I will."

"Good show, Ms. Charon," Jasper said. "I'm most excited to work with you."

"And you, Mr. Bonaparte."

He slid her banknotes. She nearly passed out at the money in her palm. She had never seen so much in one place in her life. And it was a good thing too, because the copy editor savings paying for her apartment were running pitifully low since quitting her job.

"Return to me in eight weeks' time, and we can discuss another five-paper purchase," he said as he walked her from his office.

Alton stood when she noticed Armmie and Jasper return.

"Bonaparte, good to see you," Alton said.

"And you, old chap." Jasper smiled. "Perhaps we can get a few society members tonight, eh?"

"Perhaps."

"Plan to meet at Ms. Taylor's around eight? I shall inform her she is hosting," Jasper said.

"That's hardly necessary," Alton began.

"I've already sent her a message," Armmie said. "See you this evening."

Jasper waved and shut the door of his office.

Alton turned to Armmie.

"You've spoken to Rocketta?"

"Sure. She insisted that I contact her when I returned to London. It is the least I could do, seeing as she got me this new position."

Alton clenched her jaw; for the briefest moment, she looked... Jealous?

"Very well, Ms. Charon."

"Alton..."

"Anne Marie Charon, I thought I told you I never wanted to see your face again," came a growl from behind. There in the doorway stood the cross and petulant Mr. Grue, her former employer.

"Mr. Grue," Armmie began. "I'm—"

"I figured your opportunity of a lifetime was just some scheme," Mr. Grue bit out, "no heiress would ever choose your lazy work ethic. So, as I said before, no! You can't have your job back!"

Alton looked at Armmie. Armmie looked at Alton.

"Shall I go get Jasper?" Alton asked under her breath.

"Mr. Grue, I'm here because Mr. Bonaparte is buying some of my work," Armmie said.

"Yeah, right. And I'm the King of England." He scowled. "Get out of here before I have security dump you in the street."

"That won't be necessary, Jonathan," Jasper said, a twinkle in his eye. "Why don't you join me in my office?"

Mr. Grue looked as if a ghost had shot him through the chest.

On the street, Alton looked over Armmie, as usual with her ever-scrutinizing gaze.

"You spoke to Rocketta?"

"Yes, Alton, is that a problem?"

"Why did you do it?"

"Because she was lovely to me, and I told her I would next time I was in London. I wasn't aware I needed to ask your permission," Armmie snapped.

"You don't. You don't."

There was something she wasn't saying. What was that? Less clear.

"You aren't jealous, are you?"

Alton crossed her arms.

"No. I'm not."

"Good. Then let's do something fun today. Unless you'd rather go back to my hovel and sulk."

"That's unnecessary, Anne Marie."

"Oh, don't you start."

"I was wondering what Armmie was short for."

They began walking along the River Thames.

"My childhood best friend gave it to me. She thought it was more interesting than Anne Marie."

"I would say I prefer it as well."

Then they walked in silence for a while, overlooking the city being constructed, the children playing in the streets, and the taxicabs, the birds along the cobblestones. Alton's hands brushed Armmie's as their arms hung at their sides. She did that on purpose. Armmie could tell because it was not a brief bump, but a lingering touch.

They made their way to a row of large townhouses, Alton guiding Armmie along.

"Which of these would you like, if you could have any?" Alton asked.

"That one," Armmie said definitively.

It was a beautiful two-story, with red bricks and large windows, and a little garden in the front.

"What about this one?" Alton asked of the largest house on the block. The trees blocked most of the building from their view on the street, but Armmie could tell it would be stunning.

"It's quite impressive," Armmie said.

"Would you like to go in?"

"Well, sure, in theory. Though I'd prefer not to ruin our day by being arrested for breaking and entering."

Alton jingled a set of keys.

"Why don't we check it out?"

"Do you know the owner? Don't you think it's a little inappropriate to go into someone's home uninvited?"

"I am the owner. I invite you."

"What?" Armmie exclaimed. "This is your house?"

"It is my family's. So yes."

"Alton! If you own a massive townhouse, why on earth would we sleep in my little shack?"

"Because I wanted to see where you live."

Armmie rolled her eyes.

"Unbelievable."

They entered the house, and though the air was stale, the ornateness of this building blew Armmie away. Crown molding, pillars, velvet wallpaper, silk furniture. No matter which way Armmie turned, it seemed more luxurious than the moment before.

"And I thought the manor was crazy," Armmie muttered.

"Yes. You can see why I spend less time here," Alton said.

"I can't see in the slightest! Why wouldn't you want to spend all your time here?"

"Perhaps I am afraid of the ghosts in these walls."

"You really expect me to believe that you are afraid of ghosts?"

Alton looked amused.

"What's say we play a little dress-up and go for tea?"

"Seriously?"

"Why not?"

"It just seems out of character for you to be suggesting something fun."

"I'm full of surprises, am I not?"

"Evidently."

So they donned strange Victorian attire, Armmie in a petticoat and gown, with a hand-embroidered bodice, and Alton in a ruffled shirt and peacoat.

"Do we look too ridiculous?"

"Just ridiculous enough. Let us take the trolley."

Armmie and Alton found themselves in a comically gigantic hotel atrium with a flowing champagne fountain, and all the waitstaff wore tuxedos. A live harpist played as the pair received tower after tower of little bites of food. They drank tea until they were so full that the corset Armmie wore threatened to burst.

"It was my fault for wearing something that likely belonged to an underfed woman of the time."

"You look wonderful."

"The same could be said of you, my lord."

"Why, thank you, my lady."

The pair decided they were too full for dinner and instead went to see a picture. It was called *Tapping on Melancholy's Door*, a comedy about a tap dancer with a depressed neighbor named Melancholy.

Afterward, of the film, Armmie said:

"That Finnian Arnopole sure can act."

"My money is on Celeste Valentine for this awards season."

Finally, they returned to Alton's enormous townhouse.

"Get me out of this dress."

"This again?"

"What do you want from me? It's a corset."

"Turn around," Alton said.

Armmie did. She felt Alton's dexterous fingers unlacing the corset with shocking speed.

Armmie turned around to face Alton.

"You were too good at that for someone who doesn't wear dresses," Armmie said, "who else have you been disrobing?"

Alton's gaze steeled over. It was almost remarkable the way Alton could shut down.

"It is unimportant."

"Fine. I won't push."

"That's a surprise."

"And now why is that?"

"Because you have an incessant need to know everything."

"Perhaps I just have an inquisitive mind. Is that so wrong?"

"It just always seems to be about me."

"I think you underestimate how much I keep to myself."

"If that is how much you keep to yourself, then I am beyond impressed at your dental dam."

"Where shall I change?"

"I will show you to your room."

Was Armmie disappointed she would not be sharing a room with Alton this evening? No... but if she were, she would never admit it.

The room itself was straight out of a novel. Or French royalty, from what Armmie had heard. Obviously, no one ever brought her around their château. Except, of course, Alton.

"I declare I'll get ready for the party this evening."

"I'm unsure if I'll be joining you, in truth. I'm feeling quite tired and think perhaps a bit of rest might do me well."

"You can't be serious."

"I'm afraid I am."

"And what am I to tell your friends?"

"They are your friends now, too, Armmie dear."

Dear.

"What if it's a sacrifice? What if they are luring me in to turn me into a stuffed doll or drink my blood or something?"

"They aren't going to do that," Alton said with clipped words. There was something in her eyes that was unreadable. But very dark.

"Relax, Alton, it was a joke. Seriously, I won't have any fun unless you come," Armmie said.

"I won't be going. But you ought to enjoy yourself."

And that was that.

Armmie dolled up while a reserved Alton sat on the couch, half reading a book, half looking into the cold, empty fireplace.

Only when Armmie was ready to go, and Phillip had pulled the car round, did Alton look at her.

"I'll see you tonight," Armmie said.

"Yes," Alton replied.

She adjusted the collar of Armmie's dress. Whose dress she was wearing was actually a mystery; she just found it in one of the million closets in the townhouse. Alton's fingers brushed against her neck like little zaps of lightning. Armmie shivered.

"You look lovely," she murmured.

"It's not too late for you to come with me."

"Be wary of anything they offer you. It'll be top shelf and stronger than you imagine."

The tightness on Alton's face was unreadable. What on earth was it?

"Thank you, Phillip," Armmie said, stepping out of the car.

"When shall I return for you, miss?"

"Jasper offered to drive me home," she replied.

Phillip raised a brow.

"Make sure the man can walk in a line before you get in his car," Phillip said offhandedly.

"Of course. Thank you for your concern."

Armmie could hear the thump of music from down the steps of the massive house. Shadows inside seemed to flicker through the curtained windows. She hiked up the steps and past the columns that lined the entry.

A man in a black coat held the door open for her.

"Thank you very much," Armmie said, and then realized how strange it was to have another person open her door. She understood why Alton did not keep waitstaff in her home.

As soon as the large oak door opened, Armmie saw the bacchanal before her. She stepped inside, and a crowd of at least fifty impeccably dressed people greeted her immediately, holding champagne flutes and food that Armmie had never seen before. Music wafted through the air, a sweet jazz tune to which the patrons of this party were drunkenly swinging along. She looked around, frozen to the spot. This was a scene from a fantasy.

"Armmie Charon!" Rocketta cried from behind her. "It's you!"

Armmie turned around to face her. Her cropped hair looked elegant tonight in a regal sequin dress. She held a cigarette in one hand and a flute of golden champagne in the other.

"It is indeed," Armmie replied.

"Where is Alton? Pulling the car around?" she joked.

"No, she was under the weather and couldn't make it."

"I wish I could say I was surprised."

"I take it this is not a first."

"And it won't be a last, I imagine. It was impressive to see her for so long at the symposium."

"She does so enjoy her academic pursuits."

"Well, darling, come with me. The others are in the den." Rocketta pulled Armmie along.

"And you just threw this party together? On such short notice?"

"I have nothing so fun to do! It was just a few quick calls."

Something told Armmie that Rocketta only had fun things to do, but that was beside the point. They elbowed their way through partygoers and made it into Rocketta's sitting room. What it lacked in size, it made up for in grandeur. Frescoes adorned the vaulted ceilings. Massive rugs covered the checkered tile floor. And on the silk couches sat Jasper, Cornelius, Reginald, and several others whose names Armmie never got.

"Look who joined the party," Rocketta beamed, gesturing to the rather sheepish Armmie.

"Armmie! As I live and breathe." Reginald laughed.

"We heard you had a wonderful meeting with dear Jasper," Cornelius said.

"The rumors are true," Jasper said.

Then he dragged his nose along the white powder off a silver dish on the cherry wood coffee table.

"WOO! There we are!" he exclaimed.

"Where is Alton?" Reginald asked.

"Not coming," said Rocketta.

They all looked around at one another.

"Fifty marks to you, Jasper."

"We could only be so lucky." He laughed. "I had hoped not."

"Wait a moment. You all didn't want her here?" Armmie asked.

More glances.

"Tyner.. She's a little..." Cornelius began.

"Well, she's not everyone's cup of tea," said Reginald.

"She's odd," Rocketta said politely.

Armmie thought back to what Alton had said just the night before. About her parents. About her siblings. About how she had lived such a powerful lie. How she was so alone.

"I like odd," Armmie said.

Jasper laughed and said, "Everyone is entitled to their opinion, but tonight we celebrate she stayed home."

"Jasper! Keep it to yourself," said Rocketta.

"The poor girl's got to go back to her, does she not?" Jasper asked.

"Mr. Bonaparte, why did you insist she join us if you didn't want her here?" said Armmie.

"Let us not waste another second on a person who did not deign to join us," Cornelius said.

"Hear, hear," said Reginald, "now come over and put your nose in this powder."

"What is it?" asked Armmie.

"Something you're going to love," Cornelius said.

"Hand imported from the Americas," said Jasper, going in for another snort.

Armmie remembered Alton's warning. But then again, Alton was notably absent.

"Don't do it like them," said Rocketta, "they are positively barbaric."

She opened up a little baggie from a pouch in her ample, ample bosom, and a tiny silver spoon.

"Let me show you what you're going to do."

She dipped the spoon into the baggie, lifted it to her nose, and elegantly sniffed.

"Your turn."

Rocketta filled the spoon with the white powder and put it up to Armmie's nose. She plugged Armmie's other nostril. *Now or never*, Armmie supposed, and inhaled deeply. The first thing she noticed was the odd sensation, like snorting granules of dust. She had the urge to sneeze, but lost it in the burn that came next.

"Oh!"

"Just ride the wave, darling," Rocketta advised, "let us dance."

They moved to the dance floor, where the hedonistic affair was in full swing. Armmie suddenly felt her entire body alight. She became vibrant and alive, so very alive. Rocketta was an excellent dancer.

She was pulling and swinging, and dipping Armmie. Everything felt so simple. Everything felt so free. At some point, Cornelius, Reginald, and Jasper came and danced with them until they began kissing each other. And not tender kisses, but deep, thorough kisses that were wet and sloppy, and lustful. There was tugging and groping, and eventually they were pouring champagne on one another.

"Join us, ladies." Jasper grinned as Cornelius and Reginald kissed his neck.

"We will have to pass, boys," Rocketta said. "I have my eye on someone else tonight."

Armmie had an unmistakable feeling Rocketta was talking about her.

"Oh? And who might that be?" Armmie asked with an air of mischief in her tone.

"Someone quite ravishing and delicious," Rocketta said, eyeing her hungrily. "Someone I've had my eye on."

"Is it me?"

"Why, as a matter of fact, darling, it is." Rocketta grinned. She looked so unbelievable with a sheen of sweat and big eyes. Armmie wanted to smudge her lipstick with her tongue.

"I would hate to step on another's toes..." Rocketta licked her lips.

"No, you wouldn't," Armmie replied.

"How did you know?" Rocketta grabbed Armmie by the back of the neck and pulled her in, kissing her fiercely. It was not like kissing Alton. It was not like slipping under the covers after a long day. It was not soft and warm and smoky, desperate and ephemeral and raw. No, this was devious. It was starvation. They were eating each other. Rocketta's lips were plump, and her mouth was wet. Her core didn't clench in the same way; her stomach wasn't full of need; it wasn't the release she had been craving for months now, but it was quite good. Rocketta's hands ran through her hair, squeezed her ass, and tugged her in again and again. The music throbbed in Armmie's ears as they were pushed around by the dancing strangers. Eventually, Rocketta pulled away. Armmie, now flushed, noticed that Cornelius, Reginald, and Jasper were watching in awe. And so clearly was something in their pants.

"What do you think?" Rocketta whispered. "Should we let them in?"

Armmie smirked. It would be foul. It would be debaucherous. It would be unlike anything she had ever done. But she only thought about a certain feeling in that certain area, and how much she was feeling it. Furthermore, she had drunk more than she ever had in her whole life. The room spun in a most delightful way, as though she were walking through a dream.

"Let me take us to my special room, and you can decide," Rocketta murmured.

"Wait! I have to tell Alton I'm not going home," Armmie hiccuped.

"Come with me," Rocketta said, "boys, go to your room."

Rocketta brought her to a hallway with a strange phone machine.

"I believe I have her number," Rocketta said, dialing. There was a ringing and then—

"Hello?" Alton's voice came through the little cups on the C.

"Alton?"

"Armmie? Are you all right?" Alton asked. "Is Phillip almost there?"

"Alton! I am... not joining," Armmie slurred. "Spend the night here."

"Oh."

The line was empty. There was something in Alton's voice that, if Armmie were sober in any way, might have been detected as dejected sadness. But she was not sober, so she did not detect it.

"Night night," Armmie said.

"Armmie, be safe," Alton cautioned.

"Safe sh-mafe."

"Armmie?" called Rocketta. "Are you ready?"

"Is that Rocketta?"

"Must go, Alty. See you in the morning."

And then she hung up the phone. Armmie craved and desperately wanted to see what was in this special room Rocketta had mentioned. She allowed herself to be led down an impossibly long hallway to a set of dark doors. Rocketta knocked three times.

"Are you decent?" Rocketta asked through the door.

"No," said Cornelius.

"Perfect."

Rocketta marched Armmie into the room to a massive four-poster canopy bed that had silk ropes hanging from it. The room was lit by hundreds of candles. And on the bed lay the gentlemen, naked and covering only their genitals with the loose red sheets.

"Ready?" Rocketta murmured, running a hand down Armmie's spine. Her skin prickled.

"I think so," Armmie replied in a low voice.

"Then get on the bed and take that infernal dress off."

So Armmie did. Soon she was as scantily clothed as the rest of them, losing herself in a whirlwind of mouths and fingers and cocks and the wetness down Rocketta's legs that was sweet to the taste. At some point, she felt something at the entrance to herself.

"Not there," she said, and whatever it was moved.

There was hair, smooth, soft, and coarse. There was stubble and lips and flaps and shafts. Then her hands were tied to a post as Rocketta was on her face, and Jasper was between her legs. On and on the night went, the dance having acts, having highs and lows. She was on her back, then on all fours, bent over the bed, feeling something missing, before falling asleep, sticky, wet, and exhausted.

The morning light came searing into her shut eyelids like a magnifying glass in the sun. As soon as her eyes opened, she realized exactly what had happened. Then the headache started. Then her stomach churned. Then she was coughing and sputtering and vomiting in a toilet, cold and naked. Her throbbing head rested against the seat when she heard the door creak open, to reveal Rocketta in a fluffy bathrobe.

"How are you doing, champ?" she trilled.

Armmie just groaned. Wretched. And looked up at Rocketta, who looked shockingly put together given the events of the following night.

"How... do... do you have makeup on?"

"You get used to it, darling," she said, "let's get you showered up, and I'll show you my little trick."

Armmie had to wash with her head against the tile of the shower wall for fear of passing out. Rocketta insisted she should stay, to make sure nothing happened, but it seemed like the reality was she just wanted to see Armmie naked.

"Did last night really happen?" Armmie asked, putting her hair up in a towel.

"Well, of course. Don't tell me you're having regrets."

Was she? She hadn't processed that far.

"It was quite fun," Armmie confessed. "What time is it?"

"It's 1 p.m."

"What?"

"I woke you up at 9 a.m., and you wouldn't have it."

Armmie toweled off her hair and attempted to put on her dress from last night.

"Take these," Rocketta said, handing her a pile of clothing.

"I can't very well take your clothes."

"Sure you can. You just have to promise to bring it back to me."

There was something cheeky hidden in there.

But Armmie did not want to put on her dress from last night without performing an exorcism on it, so she put on the loose trousers and large shirt when she realized her neck and chest were absolutely covered in hickeys. She looked polka-dotted. Alton would know immediately. There was a horrible conversation in Armmie's near future.

"I need to get back to Alton."

"You're always talking about her. Does she talk about you the same?"

"I... I don't know."

"Do you love her or something?"

"I don't know."

But of course she did.

"We were supposed to leave this morning."

"Why don't we get some food into you? Then you can fret about returning to your mistress."

But food sounded revolting. Jasper, Cornelius, and Reginald had all gone home. The house was empty, in fact, as if this were routine.

"How often do you have parties like that?"

"Hm. Not often. Maybe... Every other week?"

"That is so often."

"Is it?"

"Do you work, Rocketta?"

"I manage my family's affairs," she replied.

So not really.

"Eat some toast, Armmie, you look green."

Armmie ate some toast. She sucked down water as if she had just returned from a hiking trip through the desert, then had to grip the table to keep the water down. How it was possible to feel seasick on land was beyond Armmie.

"Try this," Rocketta instructed, pulling a small yellow vial from her dress pocket.

"What is it?"

"Best not to ask questions. But I can promise it will help."

Armies uncorked the vial and knocked it back. It was bitter and burned, and Armmie coughed a bit.

"How heinous."

"It's my secret recipe, darling. Drink lots of water, and tonight you'll be right as rain."

Armmie sighed, still haunted by the headache and the souring taste in her mouth.

"Can you call Phillip to get me?"

"I'll drive you, silly girl."

Armmie smiled. Rocketta was very nice. She was very nice. And she gave her attention. And she didn't scowl or frown. She wasn't odd.

They got into Rocketta's light blue convertible, which Rocketta named "Gorgeous." The name was fitting. Rocketta chatted with Armmie the whole time, while Armmie did her very best not to ruin the white suede seats of Gorgeous.

Finally, they pulled up outside Alton's house. Rocketta was making googly eyes at Armmie. Armmie was on the verge of tears from a tension headache, but perhaps they looked sparkly because Rocketta leaned over and kissed her. It was brief, and thank goodness, because there could have been disastrous consequences had she tried to slip a tongue in. She tucked a hair behind Armmie's ear.

"I'm leaving for Italy in four days. Come with me."

"Rocketta. Let me sleep off the hangover before you try to get me on a boat."

Rocketta giggled.

"That was a fun evening, Armmie. I'm glad you came."

Armmie hadn't, for what it was worth.

Armmie had to drag herself up the stairs, clutching the wall as if she were belaying the side of a craggy cliff. She made it inside, and fortunately, it was dim indoors. She just stood there in the entryway while the surrounding air played cruel pranks on her inner ear. Then she got the sweats. She tore off the shirt, leaving only her brassiere behind.

Zombified, she trudged into the sitting room, where Alton sat reading the paper and looking at where Rocketta's car had not yet driven off. She turned her head to see Armmie standing shirtless and marred with little teeth marks.

"I know. I know. You can laugh."

But Alton didn't laugh. She just stared.

"It's a funny story about what happened—"

"Did you have an orgy with my friends?"

The question landed like breaking glass. *Oh right. Yes.* She had.

"I wouldn't call them your friends," Armmie said through a splitting headache.

Alton stood.

"What?" There was a severity in her voice. Not mock severity. Nothing playful about it.

"I didn't mean it like that."

"Then what did you mean?"

"They just...they ..."

"Spit it out."

"They had some choice things to say."

"Like what?"

"That you're odd."

Alton crossed her arms.

"So you found out the people I've been calling my friends have been deceiving me, and then you had an orgy with them?"

"I was already at the party. What did you want me to do? Turn around and come sit here with you and do nothing?"

"You didn't have to sleep with them."

"Well, it's not like you've given me any reason to think I should save myself for someone else."

"Was it Rocketta? Did you lose your virginity to her?"

"How do you know I was a virgin?"

"Because I knew."

"If you wanted my virginity, you should have taken it. But I'm not yours."

"You shouldn't have done it with her," Alton bit out.

"Why? Why on earth do you care who I do it with if you don't even want me?"

"It was cruel. It was cruel of you to do this."

"Me? Alton! I have been begging you to be with me for months, and you turn the other cheek every time I try to look you in the eye. I have needs."

Alton looked away.

"I want you, Alton. I want you. Look at me. Look. Alton. Please. Alton. Let me in. Let me love you,

Alton, please. I'm sorry. I'm sorry. I shouldn't have. I just want you. Alton, look at me."

But Alton did not. She left London shortly after, and Armmie did not go with her.

Chapter Seven

The following three days were a whirlwind of being Rocketta's lapdog. Rocketta took her shopping and dressed her in pearls and gold jewelry. They even got matching dresses. She took her to the opera, to the pictures, to a rugby game. They went to the museum together. They took a bath together. Armmie had never taken a bath before and delighted in the frothy, floral bubbles and hot water that left them both pink (Armmie substantially pinker, due to Rocketta's chestnut skin). Rocketta kissed her, massaged her, and painted her lips. She had good conversation; she asked questions; she laughed at Armmie's jokes. Armmie stayed up late chatting about their lives as girls. Rocketta's parents were in America and had been for years, drilling for oil.

It soon dawned on Armmie that Rocketta had no aspirations for her life. She was content to party, spend money, and travel. All admirable desires to have, by the way, but she cared little for thoughtful talk. She didn't read. She did like art and liked to see shows, but she didn't cook. Rocketta had every meal brought to her. And she fed Armmie grapes. Armmie had been primped and promped and fattened up.

"Come with me to Italy," Rocketta begged, "let me show you the world."

It sounded so good. The first stop was a land portion around Spain, followed by boating around Italy. Should Armmie? Could she get used to a life like this? Surely she could. She wanted for nothing. She desired, and then there it was in gold and platinum. They rode in an array of fancy cars through the impoverished streets of London. And Rocketta did some fascinating things with her tongue.

Then Armmie was on the docks with her. Rocketta's trunks had been packed and were being loaded onto the ferry. All the clothes Rocketta had purchased for Armmie lay next to Rocketta's mountain. Rocketta had her arm around Armmie's waist.

"You're going to look so good tanned." Rocketta smiled, kissing Armmie on the cheek.

"I can't go with you, Rocketta," Armmie said.

Rocketta looked at her.

"I know." She shrugged. "But I had fun."

"I did too," Armmie returned, "I had a wonderful time."

"Uncomplicated isn't for you?" Rocketta said.

"Maybe in another life. Or maybe in this one. But... not right now," Armmie replied.

Rocketta leaned in and brushed her lips on Armmie's.

"Have the most wonderful orgies for me?" Armmie held her tight.

"You know I will."

Rocketta walked away and then turned around.

"If that fool won't love you, then I will. Don't forget that."

Armmie smiled. "I won't."

And she wouldn't.

Armmie sat in her dim, shithole flat, stewing. Was it a mistake for her to stay? She had just said no to an all-expenses-paid trip around the world. What she would have done for the chance to do something like that in a past life. She should not have stayed. Or maybe she shouldn't have gone to the party. So many maybes, but one thing was for certain: she never should have let Alton go.

That's how she found herself sitting on the train carrying trunks of new wares and spoils from her week with Rocketta. The city turned to dusk, and the dusk turned to night. Then she was in the country. The lights in between the towns grew farther and fewer in between until there was darkness. There were stars in the sky when she got off the train. The cab drove up the winding hills to get to the manor house. And when they pulled in, Armmie knew that there would be no one to hold the door. So she walked up those stone steps and knocked and knocked.

She called Alton's name. She pounded until her hand was sore. She didn't care. It must have been half past midnight when the door opened.

"Armmie?" said Alton, wearing her sleep clothes.

Armmie kissed her.

There it was. That feeling. That starburst in her chest feeling. The tingly lips feeling. It was a soft kiss. And brief. When she pulled away, Alton was looking at her as if tears threatened to spill all over her cheeks. So Armmie did all she could think of and wrapped her arms around Alton. She held close. To be pressed against Alton, to be surrounded by her, it was paradise.

"I'm sorry. I never should have let you go," Armmie murmured, her mouth pressed to Alton's ear, "please forgive me."

"That's all you're sorry for?"

Oh, but of course. Alton could only hold out for so long. Armmie wrinkled her nose.

"I'm sorry for getting belligerently intoxicated. I'm sorry for having sex with your friends. I'm sorry I left, and I'm sorry I let you leave."

"Anything else?"

"What am I forgetting?"

"Wait, this is my portion," Alton said, restraining a smile, "I'm sorry I pushed you away. Just give me time."

She grabbed Armmie's many bags.

"Hopefully you didn't toss all my things into the fire."

"It has been too warm to burn anything."

"So my belongings survived."

"That they have."

The pair parted ways at the junction of their rooms. When Armmie opened the door, everything was as it had been.

Armmie unpacked all her new goodies, then got into bed. And she lay awake. The bed felt large. Too large. She stood up. She got out of bed. Opened the door. Began walking down the hallway when she ran into Alton with a sheepish look on her face.

"Getting some night air?" Armmie asked.

"I couldn't sleep."

"Shall I go to you, or you come to me?"

"I can just go back to my roo—"

Armmie grabbed Alton by the sleep shirt and dragged her back to her room. Then Armmie shut the door behind the pair. Alton was playing dumb a little. Like she didn't know the first thing about sharing a bed with someone, which clearly was not the case.

But Armmie pulled down the covers and guided Alton over. She ushered her into bed. And then got in on the other side. Now they were in Armmie's bed. Armmie kissed her forehead. And then Alton did something: she turned Armmie around and wrapped her arms around her. They slept like that, together at last.

They still had not kissed since Armmie barged back in, but they had taken to sleeping in one another's rooms. Armmie supposed she was silently agreeing to the terms of "giving it time," but found she was tired of waiting.

There was also something nagging at her. This feeling like she wanted to... say something... about the way she felt for Alton. It was rather torturous. They would be sitting at breakfast, Alton's hazel eyes staring at the paper or stirring a tea, and Armmie would see her and think it. Or Alton would be cooking dinner, a little apron tied around her front, and Armmie would think it.

Every time Alton made a quip, every time she sneezed, every time Alton did anything, Armmie was overwhelmed with this absurd urge to blurt out something rather embarrassing. But when to do it? And what if Alton didn't feel the same? What if Alton shooed her out of the house?

Armmie almost said it twelve times, to her counting. The most recent time, they sat in the seating room off the kitchen, sipping tea and eating late night cookies. They had been giggling for half an hour. Alton was telling an amusing story about a time she had gone fishing.

"Of course, my mother said fishing was for the impoverished," Alton was saying.

"My father included," Armmie interjected.

"But Reginald's brother Benedict was a part of a club at his all boy's boarding school and Reginald had just gotten a very expensive rod. I joked that he was a 'master baiter' and nobody thought I was funny."

Armmie laughed.

"I think you're very funny."

"So we went to the creek by his estate—"

"—his *estate*."

"Yes, his estate, and so we went down by the creek. They couldn't catch anything all day, and I kept trying to tell them something, and they wouldn't listen. We were just about to head back when Reginald's rod snapped down. And they were all cheering because they had finally caught a fish. But they couldn't pull it up. 'Oh, it's a big one, it's a big one,' said Benedict, and I thought to myself, *how big can it be? It's a creek.* Anywho, they try to bring up the river monster and realize it's caught on a rock," Alton said.

Armmie was enamored with her, the passion with which she told her story. Armmie could see it, little child Alton standing around while the older boys fished in the creek.

"So Benedict says he's going to go get the end of the rod from the creek, and I tried to tell him to just cut the line, but he insists. He gets in up to his waist, and when he comes out, he reeks. And the other boys are jeering, oh he smells and his clothes are stained. Now Benedict is furious, and he snaps to me, 'What did you want to say, Tyner?' And so I informed him that the creek was run off from a sewage plant," Alton then sipped her drink.

"That's what they get for not listening," Armmie said.

"My thoughts exactly."

The humor on her lips, the wry expression in the corners of her eyes made Armmie woozy.

"Do you have any stories like that?" Alton asked.

"None so adventurous," Armmie said, "perhaps the best I could say is one time one of the boys in class kept making barfing noises and my teacher wouldn't listen. I kept trying to tell her and she wouldn't listen, and then he got sick on her shoes."

"Serves her right."

"My thoughts exactly."

And then there was a moment where they caught each other's eye. Armmie had performed an outstanding number on the novel *All Strung Up* by Beth Macintosh. All night, Alton's lips had been almost itching to say something. Or maybe that was wishful thinking, that Armmie desperately hoped she was holding something back. It bubbled on her tongue. The way she felt about Alton was so all-consuming she sometimes worried she had fallen ill. Alton seemed to sparkle in the moonlight. The glow of stars glittering on her face, the flickering light from the candle told stories on her perfect lips in languages Armmie could never understand.

"Alton... I—" Armmie started. Alton seemed to steel over a bit, as if she knew what would come. The flinch was a little disheartening, despite it being momentary.

"Do I have something in my teeth?" Alton asked.

"I thought so. But no."

Alton looked away. Awkward. But Armmie should know better than to think Alton would be accepting of big emotions. She wouldn't be discouraged. If she wanted Alton, seduction would have to be the way.

After Armmie's report some evenings later, she dragged Alton by the sleeve across the lawn and garden. The moon shone high in the sky.

"Tell where we are going," Alton said.

"No. And stop being so demanding."

The cicadas were chirping, and frogs were ribbiting when they made it to the lake behind the manor. Alton seized up. Armmie had taken into consideration this fact.

"Armmie, this is the lake," Alton whispered.

"I know."

She kept leading Alton along the rocky pathway until they made it to a shore with a blanket and a picnic lit by candles.

"What is this?"

"It's a picnic."

Alton rolled her eyes.

"Why have you done it?"

"We must spice things up, Alty. Delight with me, why don't you?"

Alton grinned with her eyes because, of course, doing it with her mouth would give too much away, and sat on the blanket.

"And where did you find all these supplies?"

"That manor house of yours has just about everything in it. Now dig in."

Alton seemed a bit reserved, continuously looking over her shoulder at the lake.

"I keep expecting to see him walking out."

Armmie put her arm on Alton's leg.

"I watched through the window as they threw him in. It was February, and the snow was fresh. As soon as he walked through the door, I knew he was going to die. He turned blue underwater. I tried to get him by the fire, but they locked me in the cellar."

A little tear trickled down Alton's cheek. The night was warm. Armmie kissed it away.

Alton sniffled.

"Enough of that," she trained her voice, "let us enjoy this lovely feast you've arranged."

Armmie had prepared little pastries and chilled wine. They ate and drank merrily.

"I fear I've been talking too much about myself these days," Alton began.

"You've got much time to make up for," Armmie replied.

"What were your dreams as a child?"

"My dreams?"

"Yes. What were they?"

"That may be one difference between us. When you grow up as I did, you don't really have dreams. You just hope you have enough to put food on the table, and maybe a good person to do it with."

"And who was your good person?"

"I always pictured it to be a man."

"That was your first mistake."

"Hmph. Well, I pictured him to be strong and noble, and caring. I wanted him to help me do the wash, to pick me up when I was down, to sweep me off my feet. I wanted someone who would cook me meals and keep me safe. More than anything, I just wanted someone whom I didn't have to force to love me."

"Have you ever been in love?"

"Never before."

"Did you truly lose your virginity in an orgy?"

Armmie covered her face.

"Please don't remind me." Armmie laughed.

"Was it bad?" Alton inquired.

"Do you really want to know?"

"Yes."

Armmie raised an eyebrow.

"It was quite exceptional. My sobriety obviously compromised my memory, so I can't recall any specific details, except that I believe someone tied me down at some point."

Alton flushed.

"You're not picturing it, are you?"

"No."

She was.

"And with Rocketta?"

"Are you truly certain you want to know?"

"Yes."

She was.

"It was better than when I do it myself, but... but that moment at the end... when you know you've finished... it never came. Not with her."

"Never, did you say?"

There was something fiendish in Alton's eyes.

"Does that matter to you at all, Alton? Certainly it wouldn't to the grantor of a scholarship."

Alton was red in the face.

"I'm quite warm," she said, "shall we go for a dip?"

Hm. How interesting.

"I'd be delighted, but I haven't brought us anything to swim in."

"Then I suppose you'll have to either swim in your clothes or nothing at all."

"And what will you be swimming in this evening?"

Alton began unbuttoning her shirt, sliding it off her shoulders, revealing a brassiere underneath. Alton moved to Armmie and unbuttoned the front of her dress as she lay back on the blanket, one tantalizing button at a time. Was Alton on top of her right now? It was possible. But it didn't seem real. She unbuttoned all the way down, and Armmie's dress spread in half over her reclined body. Alton stifled what could very well have been a moan as she feasted on Armmie's body. Armmie stood, both now in their underwear. They had been here before, hadn't they? This time, Armmie wouldn't hesitate.

Armmie reached around Alton's brassiere and unhooked it. She hitched another breath as the fabric left her chest. Then she was bare. Alton stepped close, and Armmie held her breath as Alton pinched her fingers on the sides of Armmie's underwear and tugged them down, so slowly. Slowly, as if she were watching an ice cube melt down a warm slide. Every revealed inch threatened to drive Armmie crazy. Alton knelt as she pulled and placed a devious kiss on Armmie's naked inner thigh, dangerously close to that now entirely revealed certain area. Armmie desperately wanted to blush or cover herself, but the only thing she wanted more was to see Alton naked.

She tore off Alton's drawers and her own brassiere, and just as she was about to reach in and kiss Alton furiously, Alton ran down the dock on the lake and jumped. Armmie had no choice but to follow after.

Moments later, she was airborne, plunging into the cool lake. When she came up for air, there was Alton, staring at her with a look in her eye that was some combination of lust and something a little more sentimental. Gentle. Caring. But the lust won out. She swam to Armmie, and as soon as Armmie caught her breath, she kissed her. How good it felt. Better than cooling off the hot night air in the lake, infinitely better. There was Alton's soft mouth, her perfect lips. There were her hands in Armmie's hair, entwining and tugging. There were her hands around Alton's shoulders, there were Alton's hands tucking her hips under, wrapping Armmie's legs around her. Then Armmie was flush against her, naked. Their skin met and glided in the water.

She noticed Alton moving toward the shore, but she didn't care. She wanted Alton's tongue in her mouth. Her body was melting into Alton. Soon they made it to the sandy shore, and Alton was on top of her, pressing her into the sand as the passive waves lapped around them.

She wanted to suck Alton's soul out, to drink it. But perhaps she wanted to be on top more. She rolled Alton off her, and for a moment, confusion flickered on Alton's face. But that lasted seconds before Armmie pinned her to the sand with her wrists above her head and straddled her. Alton whined. Whined. Oh, that felt good.

Armmie's wet hair dripped down her cheeks, and she didn't care. She had sand all over, and she didn't care. All she cared about was the feeling of being on top of Alton. Of Alton's whimper as she dragged her lower lip through her teeth. Armmie inhaled that whimper like fragrant perfume and realized she needed more of that.

It wasn't quite clear how they got back to Alton's room. She knew she had blown out the candles, but she wasn't sure if they had brought back their clothes. First, they were in the shower, and the warm water painted their naked backs. Alton pressed Armmie against the tile wall, and the cold kissed her. Her skin prickled.

Then they were on the bed.

If there had been towels on their heads, they were gone now. There would be no hair brushing, no moisturizing, none of it. Then Alton was on top again, her knee between Armmie's legs, pinning her down.

She whispered in her ear, *let me show you what it feels like to finish.* And then Alton bit her earlobe, savoring the soft skin between her teeth. Alton began kissing down Armmie's body: her neck, her collarbones, her breasts. She ran her tongue along her nipple and then down her stomach. Armmie had always imagined Alton would be a tender lover, perhaps cautious. Uneased. But Armmie was wrong. Alton was ravenous. Alton was feasting. She spread Armmie's legs wide, wider than necessary, just to take a good look.

What do you want?

Anything. Everything.

Then Alton lowered her mouth. It was like landing a plane on water. It was like catching a bouquet midair; the satisfaction of winning something she'd desperately wanted. The sensation, oh, the sensation. Armmie gripped the sheets, doing her best not to writhe around as Alton wrote psalms with her tongue. The band inside her was tightening with each kiss and suck. Something was at her entrance once more, and this time all she wanted was for it to come inside.

Please.

It came out like a beg. For food, as if she were starving. For air, as if she couldn't breathe. For sleep, when she couldn't rest. Alton's fingers pressed inside her, and a moan, a true moan, shook from the depths of her throat. This wasn't the fragmented memories of high group sex. Every moment was more vivid than the last.

Alton knew what to do.

She pumped and curled and ate until the band inside Armmie snapped. The feeling of being opened from the inside and the feeling of caress grew too much, and she shuddered again and again, convulsing on Alton Von Tyner's bed. When she ceased, Alton removed her fingers and licked them clean, a devilish smirk on her lips.

Delicious.

Alton seemed to go in for some kind of round two, but Armmie would have absolutely none of it. She had been waiting for this for months.

My turn.

Every inch of Alton's skin was delicious to the taste. It was sweeter than she could have imagined. It was like kissing satin. The little squirms from Alton drove her absolutely crazy, but she had to pace herself. Alton had made her wait. Now, Armmie would return the favor.

Armmie, I need you.

Armmie put her fingers in Alton's mouth.

Hold still.

After spending decadent seconds twirling the fingers of her other hand up and down the soaking wet slit of Alton's *certain area*, Armmie could resist no more. She dove in. Alton's soft thighs rubbed against her ears as she devoured. This far exceeded every moment of imagination. Fantasy paled to the taste, to the smell, to the touch of Alton in her mouth and on her face. Armmie was by no means an expert, but she was certainly a quick learner. She was learning things about Alton she had never known, that no words could ever say.

Then she stopped.

Alton looked up.

Is everythin—

Armmie started again, flicking and licking her tongue. She could die here. She would be content to drown between Alton's legs. Armmie had every intention of drawing this out. If Alton could, so could she. Every time Alton seemed to reach a point of no return, Armmie stopped, until Alton was a desperate, begging mess. This was too much fun.

Please, please, please, please, please let me.

So she did. The sounds Alton made grew louder, the *oh oh oh's* more frequent, until Alton burst in her mouth like a ripe strawberry. Armmie locked her arms around Alton's hips and kept her tongue moving until her jaw cramped and Alton lay limp on the bed.

Then, the fizzle. The intensity of the evening brought to a climactic end. Every drop of energy was spent. Now, only the hot coals of what was moments ago a blazing fire.

Armmie lay with her head on Alton's chest, listening to her heart beating. She looked up at Alton, a faint smile on her lips.

"I love you," Armmie murmured.

And she did. She loved Alton like a stream loves the rain, like the final stitch in a sweater. She loved Alton like a cat in the sun.

She hoped Alton would say it back, but she knew she wouldn't. Perhaps Alton felt the same, and she couldn't muster the words. Armmie could see something quite profound in her. That "I wish I could just get the words out" look in her eyes, the twitching in her lips. Alton kissed her on the top of the head. Armmie put her head back on Alton's chest. She loved Alton. For now, that would be enough.

Chapter Eight

Summer faded to fall at the manor as they passed through theology and philosophy. Armmie had learned from the greats: Donahue, Michaels, Writicus, Din, Candelas. Everybody had their own take on the makings of the universe, of how to live. Armmie was hard-pressed to find her own philosophies, searching for inspiration daily. The independent study unit was fast approaching, and she had no idea what to do. And she had come no closer to the maroon doors.

Alton remained shockingly reserved as the days came and went, rarely succumbing to the tantalizing intimacy that Armmie craved. Her restraint would be admirable if it weren't so torturous. `

She did not seem to be one for the romantics either, and so Armmie hadn't said the "L Word" since that fateful night, despite often wanting to.

Alton had since moved to painting from reading, as though she had read every book on earth—or at the very least needed a break. It seemed her studies had gone well. Soon another symposium would be in order. Armmie would often find Alton on the balcony overlooking the gardens, painting until the sky darkened. Then she would come inside, paint still on her fingertips, brow furrowed as if completely lost in thought. Armmie had tried to kiss her a few times, but it sometimes seemed like Alton's desires had minds of their own. It was difficult. She wanted to give Alton space. To give her time. But a woman has needs. She tried to say that one day. They were sitting at the breakfast nook when Armmie finally gave Alton a piece of her mind.

"Alton?"

"Armmie?"

"I'd like to talk to you about something."

"Yes?" Alton stirred her tea.

"I... I want to ... are we ever going to be... intimate again?"

Alton didn't change her expression. It was, as ever, absolutely impossible to guess what she was thinking.

"Would you like to be?"

Yes. Yes. A million million million times yes. More than anything. More than everything.

"I would."

"With me specifically?"

"No, with the other people who live here."

Alton raised an eyebrow.

"Yes, Alton. With you."

"I sometimes feel a locked door in my mind seals my desires inside. What is at times easy to open is, in other moments, quite impossible. I sit at the door, waiting to be let in. I wish that I could be. I wish I could just let the door swing open at my choosing. Perhaps to allow myself to be happy. Sometimes, it just won't open," Alton said, "but do know I'm trying to pick the lock."

"So what does that mean?"

"It means I'm doing my best to make you happy. To give you what you want."

"You make it sound like I'm asking for money."

"I don't want to hold you back from your desires. If you wish to find another person to..." Alton trailed off.

"Like Rocketta?" Armmie countered. Alton frowned.

"She doesn't live here."

"But if she did?"

"Let us not ponder on what-ifs."

"So then what? Are you trying to call it off again?"

"No, Armmie. It's not never. It's just not always."

A brief pang of sadness rang through her. The wind left her sails. Here was the woman she loved, looking so beautiful in the morning light. All she wanted was to drown herself in Alton. But Alton would not let her in once more. Oh, the torment! It never ended. Was it worth it to pursue Alton again and again if the outcome would more or less be the same? Did she want to be with someone who always chose her? It was a fairly reasonable question. But, given that Rocketta was in London, and there was nobody in this house but Alton, sometimes that would have to be enough. Besides, she made it over two decades without the touch of another person. A few months here and there wouldn't be the worst thing in the world... Probably.

...

Alton stood in the window in the morning, staring off into the garden.

"Alton, I know I've already asked you this, but please tell me the reason you spend the first hour of your day staring out this window."

"It relaxes me."

"That's all? That's the only reason you look out that window?"

"Why don't you believe me?"

"I don't know. I frankly thought that everything you did had a backstory."

"That is the backstory. I find it soothing."

"Are you looking at something?"

"No. I'm just looking at the garden. I think it's pretty."

Well. After spending all that time trying desperately to figure out the deep inner workings of Alton's mind, it seems she was once again wrong.

"Greary brought in the post," Armmie said after a moment, and with it came a thick envelope with an intricate wax seal. She handed it to Alton.

"From the Westleton Estate," murmured Alton, holding it up. She used a rather ornate letter opener and effortlessly wiggled off the seal from the envelope. She muttered to herself whatever the contents of the letter were.

"What is it?" Armmie asked, having looked up from her book, *A Discreet History of Modern Women*.

"It's from Theodore," Alton said, "I imagine it has to do with that masquerade ball he's throwing, but it's not an invitation."

Alton placed the letter in front of Armmie. Scrawled on it, in gorgeous handwriting: "Let no one see your face. 7 p.m. at this place."

"Where is the address?" Armmie asked.

"I'm not quite certain. It appears to be a set of coordinates."

"How odd."

"Why is it that such things must be so complicated?"

"Let us have a little fun," Armmie said, "have you got a mask?"

"No."

"Then we must either buy or make. Do you have the construction materials?"

"I do not."

"Then we will have to purchase some."

"And do you mean to say you wish to go all the way back to London?"

"Are there other places to purchase masks around town?"

"I know of a leather worker who might make some bespoke ones."

"Well, wouldn't that be charming?"

"I suppose."

"Then shall we go to town?"

"Have you finished your report? I would hate to have to—"

"I sincerely doubt you would hate to. But since you asked, yes. It's nearly finished."

"All right," Alton said, "I'll have Phillip bring the car around."

...

The afternoon was bright and fresh, with tree leaves fading to flame and caramel. Alton wore a burnt-umber sweater and tan trousers. Armmie walked alongside her in an orange dress.

"It should be around here."

And then they stumbled upon it: Louis's Leather.

The pair entered the shop, with a little tinkle from the bell above the door, and the smell of leather immediately overtook Armmie. She wrinkled her nose. It was not particularly pleasant.

"Hello?" Alton called out. Her tone was commanding. Her hands rested in her pockets. Armmie wanted to devour her. For a moment, the shop was silent. Then: a frizzled man with tufts of white hair coming off his otherwise balding head, and circular glasses balanced against a rather elongated proboscis.

""Ello?" he said, voice tinged with a French accent.

"Afternoon, sir. We were hoping to take a gander at your leather mask array."

"Oui, over to ze left. Ze back wall," he said, "my name is Louis if you need anyzing."

He went back to his busy work.

Alton and Armmie moved their way to the back wall, where indeed an array of leather face masks covered every inch. Alton tried on one that made her look like a rabbit, and Armmie like that of a bull. They donned different masks, giggling at some of the more ridiculous clown faces. They settled on a peacock with beautiful green and blue feathers for Armmie, and a rather feline one for Alton. It surprised Armmie, in truth, that Alton would choose something slinky rather than something more standoffish, like a wolf, but then again, Alton was full of surprises. On their way back to the register, Alton stopped.

"Come here," she said.

Armmie obliged her.

"What is it?"

"Put your hands out."

Armmie obliged her once more.

Alton slipped on a leather cuff, then a second one. Before Armmie could really register what had happened, she looked down and found that cuffs bound her wrists, separated only by a little metal chain.

"Did you just handcuff me?" Armmie asked, incredulous.

Alton tugged on the chain, pulling Armmie close to her. A little gasp slipped from Armmie's lips as she was quite effectively restrained.

"I like you much better like this," she murmured in Armmie's ear. Alton grabbed the chain and raised it over Armmie's head, stretching her and further immobilizing her wrists. This, too, served as an unfriendly reminder that Alton was taller than her.

"What are you doing?" Armmie hissed.

"Does this not remind you of that fateful night? When you fucked other people without me?"

"I'm sorry," Armmie whimpered. Oh, how pathetic. Whimpering? Unbelievable.

"No, you aren't."

"You ladies all right back zere?" questioned Louis. Armmie's face burned. It was her greatest hope in the world that he could not see them through the shelves.

"Quite," Alton called back. She turned back to Armmie and effortlessly fingered the cuffs off.

"Go wait outside, Armmie," Alton instructed, her voice so sensual Armmie couldn't argue.

Armmie was desperate to talk back. To insist that she should stay in the store. But her feet walked her right outside. And she stood outside Louis's, an unpleasant, light throbbing between her legs. Alton seemed to love stringing her along. Or some strange combination of giving and withholding pleasure on a whim. Armmie was a fish on a hook for Alton Von Tyner.

Alton returned rather smug, a jaunt in her step as she exited the store.

"Did you buy the cuffs?" Armmie asked.

"I'm sure you would love to know."

"I would, in fact, Alton."

"That inquiring mind of yours again."

Alton put her hand on Armmie's lower back and guided her down the street to where Phillip had pulled the car around.

...

Armmie was still tense at dinner. She hadn't shaken off that tenderness. The need.

"How, pray tell, are we going to find out where the coordinates lead?" Armmie asked.

"I will locate some maps."

"You've just got them lying around?"

"Something like that."

Alton sipped some of her wine. She looked so regal at the other end of the table that Armmie just desperately wanted to jump her bones. Never had Armmie been this stupidly desperate about anyone or anything. She had spent her whole life being composed and reasonable, not ever going out and drinking—mostly because that would be an unnecessary waste of money—but that was beside the point. Armmie had never lusted, never coveted. By all means, she was innocent as a lamb. And then this advertisement in the paper happened across her desk, and suddenly, she was a fool for a statue of a woman. She wanted to be the bite of food on Alton's fork.

"You're silent this evening."

Her mind was not, however.

"I'm lost in thought."

"Oh, are you now? And what about?"

Foul and filthy things that had to do with a certain new acquisition from a certain store.

"Wouldn't you like to know?"

"Armmie. If there's something you'd like to say, you ought to just spit it out."

Armmie pushed the food around on her plate a bit. A pot pie of mushrooms and red wine. It was exceptional, as always.

"No, no. Nothing at all."

How do you like it, Alton? Armmie wanted to spit. But by some wickedness within Alton, it seemed she knew Armmie was putting up a front to goad her into revealing what her plans were with those leather cuffs.

"Well then. Should we get on our way to your report?"

Alton would be the death of her, Armmie decided.

In the sitting room, Alton lounged with a devious look in her eyes.

"What Maliopia does well in *Saints of the Sun* is bring forth the idea of classical divinity into a more contemporary lens. The protagonist is not a singular person, but in fact an entire church, leading the reader to question where a group of humans can be good. I found it intriguing, especially considering Maliopia herself was often seen as a saint in her time. That said, she seems to criticize herself by being so scrutinizing of this religious sect."

"Did you enjoy it?"

"I was rather fond of it, as a matter of fact."

"Well, Armmie, I must say I am duly impressed. I find this is one of your best reports."

"Sincerely?"

"Sincerely."

Alton stood and maneuvered the secretary desk, that was against the wall, to the center of the room. Then, she pulled over a cushioned chair and sat Armmie down in it.

"Now, what is this about?" Armmie inquired.

"I'd like you to write lines."

"Lines? Isn't that some form of archaic punishment?" Though famously, Alton was no stranger to dishing those out.

"Not always." Alton placed a notepad in front of her and an ink pen to the side. At the top of the page was written, "Good Work is Rewarded."

"Alton, what is this?"

"You are to write this line until you finish."

"Finish? And when will that be?"

"I suggest you begin now."

Armmie rolled her eyes. Yet she, as ever, found she could not say no. Armmie pressed the pen to the paper and wrote the first word, when Alton knelt on the floor and crawled under the desk. Armmie stopped writing.

"What on eart—"

"Keep writing, Ms. Charon."

Armmie rolled her eyes until she felt hands roll up the sides of her skirt, pull off her underwear, and widen her legs.

"Alton!"

"Now, Ms. Charon."

The command was just too much. Armmie put the pen back on the page and began writing the second word when she felt Alton's tongue caress her inner thigh. She wrote the third word, then 'Rewarded' when Alton pressed a kiss to the epicenter of the throbbing.

A wave of indescribable pleasure washed through her as her left hand gripped the desk and her right continued onto the second line. Soon enough, little moans broke through Armmie's labored breath. She had reached line number fifteen when Alton picked up the pace, and twenty when her toes curled. She felt Alton dig her nails into the outsides of her hips and thighs, holding her in place. Onto line twenty-five, and the tension within her grew too much as she panted Alton's name. She came moments later. Alton's kisses grew slower and slower until that wash of pleasure subsided, and she stood out from under the desk, wiping her face on a handkerchief.

"Let's see."

With shaky hands, Armmie held out the page.

"Twenty-seven. Good work," Alton said.

"Good work is rewarded," Armmie replied, a little faint.

"What a quick learner you are."

Alton leaned in, placing her lips right by Armmie's ear.

"You are such a good girl when you want to be."

Armmie shuddered.

"I was going to offer to go through those coordinates and try to locate where dear Theodore would like us to go, but perhaps we can save that for tomorrow."

"Oh-oh-okay," Armmie stuttered.

"Goodnight, Ms. Charon," Alton said and strode out.

It sometimes felt as though Alton lived just to torture her. The question was, would Armmie let it stand?

Armmie was on her way to Alton's room before she could even decide on an answer. She knocked on the door and waited. And waited some more. Then she knocked again.

"Alton. Open the door."

Nothing. Very well, thought Armmie, before putting her hand on the door and pushing it open. In the room, Armmie found Alton on her bed, one hand under the covers.

"Alton!"

Alton stopped and immediately looked sheepish. Alton, sheepish.

"What are you doing here?" Alton asked, face still reddened.

"I could ask you the same thing, old lady."

"I'm —"

Armmie stormed over to the bed where Alton lay.

"It is so unbelievably disrespectful that you would do this without me, after what you did this evening."

How good it felt to be the one chastising. What a dream.

"Bend over the side of the bed," Armmie commanded.

She was trying out her Alton voice. For a moment, Alton seemed to contemplate whether she would obey. Would Alton decide to play along?

"Armmie, I'm not going to—"

"Now."

There was a hint of a scowl on Alton's face as she shuffled lower to the side of the bed and draped herself over it.

"This is highly unnecessary."

"Quiet, Ms. Tyner. And watch your manners."

Armmie spotted the handcuffs on Alton's nightstand. Absolutely perfect. She picked up Alton's hands on either side of her and placed them on her lower back before slipping both wrists into the cuffs. Alton was rendered immobile. Finally.

Armmie tugged down the sleep shorts that Alton wore, though she could tell they were already soaked through. Then, Alton was bound and spread over the edge of the bed. So this was what Alton had been doing to her. Suddenly, everything made a little more sense. It was a glorious view. Armmie ran her fingers along Alton's inner thighs, then over what was indeed her soaked slit so lightly, just barely more than a tickle.

Alton squirmed. She struck Alton's right upper thigh, watching as the faint stroke of pink bloomed where her hand had met skin seconds before. Alton gasped and feigned trying to writhe free. Armmie would not be wasting her time doing that. No, she had far more pressing matters to attend to. So she knelt at Alton's feet and placed her mouth right on what Armmie had recently learned was her clitoris. Then she kept her mouth shut until Alton finished.

...

Armmie was taking her tea in the sitting room when Alton arrived, hair tucked up in her ever-tight French twist. Today, she wore a navy pin-striped shirt, under a navy wool sweater vest, navy pants, and a little neck kerchief tucked in.

"Why so formal?" Armmie asked, noticing how shabby she felt in comparison.

"Formal? This isn't formal." Alton chuckled. She had long paper tubes under her arm.

"What have you got there?"

"Maps."

Alton placed them on a table and smoothed them out.

"Where on earth did you get maps?"

"I had them lying around."

"Do you store them in the library?"

Alton's expression immediately changed.

"No."

Her mouth was a hard line.

"Why can't I know whether there is a library in this house?"

"Armmie. Let it go."

"Is that what's behind the maroon doors?"

Alton took a step back.

"I don't understand, Alton! It's just a library. You don't have to be so secretive."

A sense of dread washed over Armmie as she realized perhaps she was not doing the right thing.

"I will ask you one more time to forget this and move on."

The urge was there. The urge to let it go. Then, the urge to fight. To know. Armmie was torn.

"Alton..." Armmie tried to do some puppy-dog eyes. Some lower lip pouting, some quivering, some eyelash batting, but Alton was completely and entirely unmoved. And something darker, too. There was anger in her eyes. There was tension in her jaw. Her arms were crossed, fists tight. It dawned on Armmie that if she pushed, if she continued on her seemingly futile quest to find out Alton's secrets, Alton might shut her out for good. Perhaps Armmie would just have to find out for herself. She sighed.

"What are the maps for?"

The tension in Alton loosened a bit. Little by little, her glacier melted.

"They are of town," Alton said, smoothing out one, "And this is all the neighboring towns from here to London."

"Are you going to cross-reference the coordinates from the invitation?"

"That's correct."

Alton placed a magnifying lens on the map and began sliding it around, glancing at the invitation from time to time.

"Can I help?" Armmie asked.

Alton shook her head, muttering and moving the glass. Finally, she stopped.

"Here." Alton pointed to the map. "The Wicken Forest."

"How spooky," Armmie said.

"Just in time for All Hallows' Eve."

Armmie looked at Alton thoughtfully. She looked so good in that sweater vest; it was unbelievable.

"Shall we pick out our clothes?"

"You were going to wear something more than your regular clothes?"

"Of course," Alton clucked, "there's a whole attic of costumes in this house."

Armmie remembered the moment Alton saw her in the white dress.

"Am I allowed back?"

"Yes. You're allowed back."

"Tonight then? After dinner."

"Tonight."

...

Armmie took a walk through the gardens before dusk. Alton was standing on the patio overlooking the ground, painting once more. And Armmie, much to her dismay, was lost in thought. Oh, how she hated to contemplate. With her hands clasped behind her back, she pondered as she walked. This Alton character. She was trouble. What could she possibly be hiding? There was nothing she could show that would change how Armmie felt about her. Well... was that really true? What would it take for Armmie to see Alton differently? She mulled over the possibilities. A pile of dead bodies, perhaps? Caged animals... drugs?

No matter which way she spun it, she couldn't for the life of her figure out what Alton was hiding.

She made her way over to the cemetery. A low evening fog had crept in, and the cawing of the circling crows above the graveyard jolted her from her stupor. The grass was starting to die, but it still remained mostly green. Armmie looked through the names of the mossy tombstones. Some Von Tyners, some Archibalds, some Montigues, some Bishops. There was a plot of five at the top of the hill on the far end from the entrance. The sun was setting, painting the sky in midnight blue. She should head back. She should. Yet, Armmie walked toward the five tombstones.

When she reached the top of the hill, her breath caught in her throat. The graves of four Von Tyners. The two larger: Gregory and Eloise. The three smaller ones, George, Annie, and Alton. Though the date of Alton's death had not yet been chiseled into the rock, for obvious reasons. To think that Alton's whole family was buried here... it was terribly tragic. How many times had Alton wandered through this cemetery, waiting for ghosts to appear? Did she ever talk to them? And further, how sad that these children were in the ground because of their ghastly parents. And how grateful she was that Alton was not with them. Armmie glanced to see a bush with white roses. She went over and pulled two off, nicking herself in the process. But she didn't really care. Armmie set the flowers on the graves of George and Annie.

"I'm sorry," she whispered, as if they could hear.

The sun had almost fully descended, and soon Armmie could see her breath. She turned over her shoulder to leave when she saw Alton, and she startled. Now wearing a long camel coat and a melancholic look on her face, even in sadness, she was beautiful.

"I'm sorry I startled you," Alton said softly.

"Why did you come? I thought you were painting."

"I saw you going into the cemetery."

"And you followed me?"

Alton had her hands shoved in her pockets. Armmie couldn't seem to fit the pieces together. She did not know Alton Tyner. And yet... yet she knew a companion. She knew a friend. A lover.

"Do you miss them?"

"Every waking second."

Armmie kissed her forehead.

"I'm sorry, Alton."

"It was not you who killed them."

"Let's go back. I can make dinner tonight."

Alton nodded.

...

They dined on hot soup. Alton was a little tense, but Armmie supposed that just came with the territory. If you sail your ship on the sea, it will not always be calm. If you fly a plane, you cannot expect the sky to always be clear. Anything worthwhile had risks. At least that was what Armmie told herself. Armmie started a fire in the hearth in the living room. She ushered Alton onto the sofa and wrapped her arms around her, leaning her back to lie on her chest.

"Armmie, this is hardly necessary," Alton complained. Though notably, she did nothing to stop it. She lay on Armmie's breast. And Armmie caressed her. How she loved to caress her. It felt so good to be wrapped in the smell of wood and smoke.

"I still love you," Armmie murmured into Alton's hair. Alton squeezed Armmie's hand. It was all Armmie could hope for that Alton felt it back.

The fire burned to coals as they lay there. Alton looked up at the ceiling, and Armmie looked at her. Eventually, the fire burnt out.

"Shall we go try on our costumes?" Alton asked.

"You don't want to go to sleep?"

"It's not late."

Alton stood. She put her hand out and pulled Armmie to stand. She studied Armmie, biting her lip.

"You can say what you want to say, Alton. I will not judge you."

"Should we match?"

So not tonight.

"I think we ought to."

They were in the massive attic soon after, rifling through row after row of absurd garb. Through hats and coats and gowns, with petticoats and daggers and top hats. Ultimately, Alton selected a silver and black leopard coat, a velvet top hat, and a cane with the head of a jaguar to match her feline mask. Armmie decided on an emerald floor-length gown and a sapphire-feathered shawl.

"Do we look ridiculous?"

"Positively," Armmie replied. She looked at herself in a mirror. Here was the girl who grew up poor and alone, now dripping in plush fabric and jewels.

"What are you thinking about?" Alton asked. Armmie turned to Alton.

"I can't believe I'm here," she confessed.

"Oh?"

"This dress probably costs more than all the money I'd ever make," she said.

"Well... you might have gotten a raise in the future," Alton said a little snarkily. Armmie wrinkled her nose.

"You look ravishing, Armmie. Don't focus on the past."

"You think I'm ravishing?"

Alton rolled her eyes. Then she took Armmie's hands in her own, gently, and hummed. The soft vibrations on her lips were almost trancelike. They danced. Alton spun her, their feet twirling. They stepped forward and back, a loose waltz—though Armmie was never taught a dance of such stature— that led them across the floor of the attic, surrounded by all the clothes of past aristocrats, as if they still inhabited their old lives. The ghosts were witnesses to the back and forth, the spins and dips, and finally the gentle sway of Armmie's face on Alton's chest, Alton's chin resting atop Armmie's head. Alton paused her humming. Armmie pulled away, quizzical.

"I..." Alton pleaded with her eyes. But Armmie could not say it for her. She just brushed Alton's cheek with her thumb.

"I know."

Chapter Nine

It was another foggy night that Armmie and Alton, now masked, trekked their way through Wicken Forest. Indeed, falling on All Hallows' Eve, there was an air of spookiness that whispered through the low mist. Alton looked dashing in her leopard coat, and Armmie quite elegant in her feather shawl. They walked arm in arm—for warmth, of course. The ground was wet with fog; the trees were dark as silhouettes in the moonlight. Moss and sticks crunched underfoot.

"How far?" Armmie asked.

"Close."

Alton had meticulously copied the map onto a separate piece of paper to ensure its exactness to the original and was leading them through the dim forest with a lantern in hand.

"My feet hurt," whined Armmie.

Alton put her hand on Armmie's lower back, guiding her forward.

"Stop complaining, princess," Alton replied. In the distance, a golden tent appeared on the horizon.

"That must be it," Alton said.

They headed over. Standing by the flaps of the gold tent were two (presumably) men in matching jackal masks. Alton and Armmie tried to enter, but the men put their arms out to stop them.

"Password?" said one in a deep voice.

"Guava," Alton responded.

They had figured it out based on the letters that had pinpricks next to the corresponding letters on a scrap of paper. It had gone something like this:

˙Good Day,

˙Under the shade of ˙autumn, I'm ˙very ˙at peace.

—Theodore

Armmie had never heard of a "guava" before, but of course, Alton was the proud owner of some fantastical manual about tropical fruits and exotic birds.

The jackals nodded to each other and stepped out of the way of the tent flaps. The tent itself was empty, minus a crimson rug on the floor.

"Now what on earth is this?" murmured Alton.

"There is nothing else in here," Armmie said.

"It must be a mistake."

"Should we check under the rug?" Armmie suggested.

Alton thought for a moment.

"I don't see why not." So the pair grabbed the corner of the rug and flipped it up, revealing an oak trapdoor.

"How terribly odd," Alton said, then grabbed the brass handle and pulled it open. Under the trapdoor was a set of cobblestone stairs that led into darkness.

"Do you reckon we are going to be killed?" Armmie asked.

"I notice you think we rich people are going to kill you often."

"What else do you find entertaining besides hunting big game and doing drugs?"

"I suppose killing our party guests," Alton said snidely, "after you, my lady."

Armmie heaved a sigh and placed her foot on the top stair. Then the next. Then the next. Then, she found herself at the bottom of said stairs and entering a store hallway lit with flaming torches.

"There seems to be only one way," Alton remarked. So they walked down that one way until the sound of the party seemed to rebound off the rock walls.

"We must be going in the right direction."

Eventually, they found themselves before a dark door. Alton pulled on the handle and opened up to the most dramatic, elegant ball Armmie had ever seen. It made Rocketta's look like the most pitiful get-together in the world—no offense to her. This was absurd.

The guests were dripping in long velvet dresses, chiffon, silk, satin, and furs. The masks were elegant, handcrafted, and divine. Each person was obscured, but Armmie couldn't have recognized them anyway because she didn't know a soul here. Masked servers passed around hors d'oeuvres, and a masked band played a melancholic tune with dramatic harps and strings that Armmie could hardly even comprehend. It felt as though the band had come from heaven to perform for just the night. And then there was the party itself.

Opulent was an understatement. Luxurious was an insult. The party was so raucous, so gluttonous, it would have made Dionysus blush. There was a waltz on the floor. Partygoers dripping jewels, resplendent drapery from the vaulted ceiling of rock. There was groping and kissing, champagne bubbling like liquid gold. Soon, a flute of mysterious drink was deposited into Armmie's hand. Before she could say anything, Alton tipped Armmie's chin back, held open her mouth, and poured a little inside. Armmie swallowed. Through the mask, Alton looked ravenous. She spotted who she assumed to be Theodore and Pierre, based on stature alone, at the head of an absurdly long table covered in a feast. Armmie tugged Alton to them.

Theodore stepped off the dais, Pierre behind him.

"Tyner, you made it," Theodore said.

"I know no one of that name," Alton replied.

He bowed.

"My mistake."

"How fortunate we are that you have joined us this evening," Pierre said. "I see you found the location all right."

"Indeed, we did," Armmie replied.

"Can I interest you in some illicit substances?" Theodore asked.

"I think we will pass," Alton said, ever the picture of grace.

"You won't even remember saying yes in the morning," Pierre disapproved, "tonight you are no one but your mask."

Theodore deposited a pill into Armmie and Alton's hands.

"To pride and to onim," he raised his glass, "if you can't come in him, come on him."

Then he and Pierre threw their heads back with the pills and washed them down with the indubitably expensive champagne.

Armmie and Alton exchanged looks. Then Armmie knocked back the pill. Alton rolled her eyes and did the same.

"Blessed evening to you both," Theodore bowed again. And then he and Pierre were gone into the crowd of masked figures.

"Will Jasper and Rocketta be here?"

"You would like that, wouldn't you?" tutted Alton.

"Not because... not for any specific reason," Armmie protested.

"I'm sure. It's just the last time you found yourself under the control of unknown drugs, you had a fivesome with people you had met twice."

"We had met three times at that point, actually."

"My mistake."

"It sounds like you're jealous, Alty."

Alton flushed red.

"I am nothing of the sort. I just think it's funny."

"Oh, and that's why you bring it up twice a week? You could just let it go."

"I have let it go."

"Or perhaps you wish you could do the same. Are you curious, Alton Von Tyner, about such taboo subjects?"

Alton said nothing. She was simmering. Soon, they entered a fairytale of footsteps and masks. Armmie did her best through the blurry haze and strobing lights to monitor Alton. For long moments, they were dancing and sweating on each other. Then her mind would go blank, and she would come to. It went a little something like this:

Oysters. Sucking them down. The slimy cold. Washing her mouth out with champagne. Blink.

Being groped. Hands on her waist. Her ass. Someone pulling her hair—unclear who. Blink.

Hands against the wall of a coat closet. Fingers inside her from behind. The sound of her own grunting. Blink.

Hot wax was poured on her stomach. At some point, she had shed her dress, at least down to her hips. Blink.

Her mouth slurping hard liquor out of a belly button. Roaring laugher. Blink.

Back in the coat closet. Her leg over the shoulder of a feline. Blink.

Bent over the arm of a merlot couch. Someone's head had gone through a portrait. Someone eats caviar out of her mouth. Blink.

A massive bed. Sticky with alcohol. Panting. The candles flickered as if they were possessed. Blink. Blink. Darkness.

In the morning, she awoke with a gasp.

"Oh, mercy," she mumbled as she climbed over the naked bodies of still-masked partygoers. She slumped off the bed. The forces of gravity were working against her. She fell to the floor, bracing her hands against the Persian rug.

"Please don't..." she muttered to herself, a prayer to keep everything inside her till she could make it to a toilet. She barely passed the threshold of the restroom and threw open the lid of the bowl before hurling her guts up.

"Good morning, sunshine," Alton said.

Armmie groaned.

"How are you so... chipper?"

"A lifetime of practice," Alton said, helping Armmie off the floor.

Armmie wobbled, testing to see how putting her head over her heart would go. So far, so good.

"Don't tell me we have to walk through the forest again."

"I won't tell you if you don't want me to."

"Theodore lied about remembering," Armmie queased. "I remember all right."

"Let's get you home."

After an absolutely treacherous walk from the steps up to the trapdoor, and by the way, the tent was gone, so it was just a trapdoor in the woods, Alton ambled Armmie home. Armmie had her head pressed against Alton's chest as they walked. The spinning.

"Was this worse than the last time?"

"Infinitely."

Armmie found herself with her head resting on a rolled-up towel in Alton's tub. Alton had drawn her a bath with lavender oil and puffy bubbles. The steam rising off her was hopefully cooking all the ailments out of her system.

"How are you feeling?" Alton asked.

"I'm coming back to life," Armmie replied.

A crease of worry lined Alton's forehead. It was quite charming to see her doting, in truth. Armmie couldn't help but enjoy it.

"Do I still have to do my report tonight?" Armmie asked, like a sick child trying to get out of school.

"I believe this is report sixty-four?" Alton tapped her chin. "Do you think my ruler would survive?"

Armmie wrinkled her nose.

"Fine."

The remarkable dichotomy of snark and tenderness in Alton's eyes was ever confusing. Some time later, Armmie signaled she wished to be led out of the tub, by which point Alton presented her with a towel and turned away. Why did she refuse to look?

"Alton, don't be ridiculous."

"I will see you for dinner."

And then Alton left her own bathroom.

Armmie toweled off with the extraordinarily fluffy towel—the quality blew her mind. *Rich people*. Then, hobbled out of Alton's now vacant room, down the hall, and to her own bed that she promptly threw herself on.

She lay in bed, writing this infernal report on *Liquid Poppy* by hand, finding it not possible to sit at a desk. When she finished her report, she headed downstairs. Alton had her sleeves rolled up. Armmie lingered for a moment, lapping Alton up with her eyes.

"Go on, take a seat."

"Do you need any help?"

"For you to stop looking at me like that."

Oh, here we go. Alton was in a mood.

"Like how?"

"Like that, you're undressing me with your eyes."

"I think you're projecting."

"I'm doing nothing of the sort."

"Yet you've made comments about undressing before we even sit."

"You've come in a bathrobe to dinner this evening."

"I'm recovering."

"You could have recovered in proper clothes."

"And you could not have mentioned my taking your clothes off."

Alton leveled a gaze at her. Armmie sat. Alton raised an eyebrow, then turned and walked to the kitchen. Armmie won.

Alton placed a simple dish of stewed vegetables and rice in front of her.

"Something gentle on the stomach while you recover."

Then she sat at the other end of the table.

Armmie muscled through dinner—not because it wasn't delicious—but because the flavor of the food threatened her stomach.

"Shall we do anything this evening?"

"I assumed you would pass out after your report."

Armmie had forgotten about that.

"Yes. Most likely."

The report itself was fine; she passed, but was not rewarded for good work. Unfortunately. Alton seemed unreadable that evening. Perhaps a night of debauchery had not loosened her up as Armmie had hoped it would. Armmie dramatically pretended she couldn't get to her room; Alton helped her, and then they parted ways. Armmie wished that she had it in her to go to Alton's room. To sleep in her bed. But the moment her head hit the pillow, sleep smothered her in an instant.

…

The holiday season was soon upon them. Alton and Armmie both silently acknowledged that there would be no family dinners. Armmie suggested a holiday celebration with Jasper and Theodore and the entire crew, but Alton politely declined. They went on walks. They wore sweaters and ate cookies. They listened to the carolers in town. When the first snow fell, Armmie threw a snowball directly at Alton. The pop of white powder on Alton's face gave way to a furious glare and a handprint on Armmie's ass. Not to mention the snowball that reamed an unsuspecting Armmie in the back of the head days later.

The lake behind the house had almost frozen over. Alton seemed all right, though Armmie could not get so much as a grope out of her. There was some light pecking once in a while, but Armmie now desperately needed release.

She received a call one day on an evening that was pitch-black moments after the sun went down. The phone rang.

"Armmie darling, tell me that's you," Rocketta's voice came through the phone.

"Rocketta?"

"Indeed, it is. You have thought of me often, I hope."

"Why yes, of course. Tell me, how was your voyage?"

"Oh dear, it was wonderful. The food, the people, even the weather! I bought a beautiful brooch I would simply love to show you."

"And I would love to see."

"When are you coming to London next?"

"I have no plans to do so."

"Then make some, darling."

"I'm in the throes of academia."

"Throw the academia out for a while. Let me spoil you."

"Oh, that's not necessary."

"Nothing is necessary when you're me. Tell me, and tell me truly, is she treating you like a princess?"

Princess... not quite.

"I don't need to be treated like a princess."

"Yet you should be. I must insist."

"You are not one to be argued with."

"What if I take you both on vacation? She can study up."

"I'll discuss it with her."

"We can travel to any place you like."

"Rocketta, you are too kind."

"I'm just kind enough. Tell me when you're ready, and we can go."

Then she hung up to keep Armmie from presenting further arguments.

At dinner that night, Armmie and Alton sat on the far ends of the table.

"I spoke to Rocketta this evening," Armmie said.

Alton raised an eyebrow.

"I never should have shown you how that phone works."

"Maybe so. But the cat is out of the bag."

"What did she want?"

"To take us on vacation."

"Both of us?"

"She said you can study up."

"I can study up?"

"That's what she said."

"You're welcome to go on vacation anywhere you'd like. So long as you get reports to me twice a week."

"What if... I use my second holiday?"

"You'd like to use your last holiday?"

"Maybe."

"Well then, don't let me stop you."

"But you must come."

"Must I?"

"Why don't you like Rocketta? She's a lovely girl."

"I don't dislike her."

"You seem to be very unfond of her."

Alton chewed some of her gnocchi. Then sipped her wine.

"Armmie..."

"Alton..."

"It's just extraneous."

"Alton. I'm going to tie you up and put you in a trunk and drag you somewhere far off."

"You're going to tie me up?"

Now that was something that had crossed Armmie's mind again and again. That plus those little squirms...

"If you continue your protesting."

Armmie scraped her fork through the red sauce. Dinner had been delicious. Spinach gnocchi, handmade by Alton. Armmie had made a few while pestering her in the kitchen.

"Dinner was excellent."

"With your help."

"You appreciated my help?"

"More than being poked with your fork."

After dinner was cleaned up, they retired to the sitting room with some tea.

"Will you think about it, Alton?"

"I think about lots of things. What is the 'it' in question?"

She was obviously playing dumb.

"Holiday with Rocketta."

"It will be taken into consideration."

She felt like such a woman, but she was desperate to know, *"What are we?"*

"Alton?"

"Yes, Armmie?"

"Are you ever going to tell me if you've been in love?"

Alton shook her head.

"I don't see why it's so important for you to know."

"It's my curious mind."

"That again." Alton tutted. "Fine. An answer for an answer?"

"Deal."

"I was in love when I was younger. There was another girl at my school... well, she wasn't at my school... she worked at the pie shop across from my bus stop—"

"You took the bus?"

"Armmie, do you want to know or not?"

"Sorry."

"As I was saying, I noticed she would watch for me from the window. I believe it was her mother who made the pies. She would sit with me at the bus stop and talk about where we would go in our lives. I was rather fond of her. We were … together… in essence, for almost two years. Then my father saw us holding hands. And I never saw her again," Alton said.

"That's glum."

"So was I. I'm wondering if I have any good stories to tell you. I fear everything that comes out of my mouth makes me sound hopeless and miserable."

"I don't think that. I prefer your honesty to silence," Armmie said, "though I welcome a positive tale once in a while."

"I'd like an answer first."

"Yes?"

"Where are you going after this?"

Now there was a question Armmie had put no thought into. She had been so focused on the now, on getting Alton to open up to her, that she hadn't even considered what came next.

"I've always wanted to go to the University of Prague."

"So that's where the scholarship money will go."

Though a twinge of sadness went through her as she thought about how far away the University of Prague really was.

"Maybe."

"And what will you study?"

"My turn for an answer."

"All right."

"What will you do when I leave?"

Alton looked taken aback, like she too had not considered what would happen come the 1st of March.

"Perhaps travel."

"Oh, so you do want to travel, just not with me."

"That's not—"

"I'm going to need to go to London anyway, to pick up my pay for the most recent round of my essays…"

That, at least, had been going swimmingly well. Jasper said they were a smash hit and wanted to keep them running indefinitely. Last they spoke, neither mentioned his head between her legs, and her fingers wrapped around his—

"…We could leave from there," Armmie finished.

"I said I'll think about it."

"What is there to think about?"

"Armmie."

Something simmered in Alton's eyes. Not anger, but... Tension. It was clear that some degree of internal turmoil plagued her. There was something... The wall that Alton had built around herself was so impenetrable that Armmie had just given up on trying to scale it. Or bust it down. The best she could do was to coax it open.

Later that evening, they sat reading their books on the sofa. Armmie was reading a historical book on the fall of the Etherians. How the emperor's hubris led to the downfall of the entire civilization. What a tragic concept, to think one person could lead to the destruction of everyone.

"Alton—"

"Stop it."

"But—"

"Stop."

"You're no fun."

"You're whining like a child."

"I'm going. I'm going to go."

"Good. I hope you enjoy yourself tremendously. I will be here when you return."

Armmie slammed the book shut and moved her feet.

"Alton, I'm serious."

"Armmie, so am I."

"I don't understand your obsession with staying home."

"I went to Theodore's party, did I not?"

"I'm not going to have any fun without you."

"What a shame."

"What would it take for you to come with us?"

"I simply do not wish to."

"You're driving me crazy."

"That makes two of us."

Armmie frowned. She did not like this side of Alton. The cold. The ill-tempered. No, she preferred the wry Alton. She did not mind reserved. She didn't even mind tense. But this? Consistent refusal? It made Armmie wonder if things between them were meant to be. Which was a terrifying thought. But with only three and a half months left of the scholarship, it was unclear where things were going.

"What are we doing, Alton?"

"It looks like we are reading."

"You're being obtuse again."

"Obtuse?" Alton gritted her teeth. "Armmie, dear, I am not the one of us being obtuse."

"You refuse to answer my questions. You don't want to come out of your shell. You're content to stay in this big, empty house with your books and your library that I'm forbidden to know about. And by the way, I still don't know what's behind the maroon doors!" Armmie stood, anger overtaking her. "Rocketta says she will take care of me and spoil me, yet I still choose you even though you refuse me constantly."

Alton crossed her arms.

"Then maybe you should be with her instead of me."

"Well, that's easy to do, especially considering we aren't together."

"Enjoy your vacation. I'll see you when you return, if you even want to."

How infuriating.

"You're just going to let me go?"

"What would you rather I force you to stay? So you can resent me for all eternity?" Alton scowled.

"The only reason I would resent you is that I have given you everything and you won't even go on a goddamn vacation with me! I mean, it's not like I'm asking for your hand in marriage or to buy me a house! It'll be one week of having fun, and you still won't go! Why? Why?" Armmie was short of yelling now.

"I don't want to."

"You're whining like a child."

Alton clenched her jaw.

"Goodnight, Ms. Charon. I hope you return to finish your scholarship, but perhaps you should pack your trunks just in case."

Then she strode off, head held high. The room became crushingly empty. Armmie's vision blurred as hot tears spilled down her face. She sat on the sofa, knees pulled into her chest, and rocked back and forth. What was so troubling about this moment was that all she wanted to do was tell Alton how she felt. She cried and cried. It was pathetic and cathartic at the same time. She wanted Alton so badly. Yet to be rejected again and again... it put a strain on her. Her chest was tight. It hurt. Her eyes burned. She just wanted to feel better. After the river of tears had run dry and Armmie had most graciously wiped all the snot off her face, she marched back to the kitchen. The phone rang twice.

"Rocketta?" Armmie said, voice wobbly.

"Armmie, darling, what's happened? Are you all right?"

Armmie couldn't get into that now.

"Where are we going?"

"Hm?"

"Where are we going for holiday?"

"I'm thinking Cairo, darling. Will Alton be joining?"

A little cry slipped out. She tried to sniff it back up.

"I don't believe so."

"I'm unsurprised. Give me a day, Armmie. I'll have a driver pick you up the morning after tomorrow, and we will be off."

"Thank you, Rocketta."

"Don't thank me, Armmie. Now rub those tears into your face. They're supposed to make your skin dewy."

Armmie chuckled. Then the phone line went dead. She massaged the tears into her face, feeling quite silly doing so. She put a pot of tea to boil. Moments later, she had poured herself a cup. The house felt so empty.

The following day was the same. Alton was nowhere to be found until dinner.

"I'm leaving tomorrow morning," Armmie said curtly, as Alton dropped her plate in front of her.

"I hope you have a wonderful trip."

That was insincere.

"You're still not coming?"

"You'll have more fun without me."

So that's what this was about.

"You're wrong."

Alton turned to her food, stabbing her fork around absentmindedly. She looked up at Armmie with something on her face Armmie just couldn't place. Wounds. Wounds that went back to when Alton was a child. Heaviness in her eyes. Weights on her lips. That perfect face, sunken.

"When did you first start thinking that people would rather be without you?"

Confusion flashed across her face.

"I don't know."

Her jaw seemed fused. But Armmie held her gaze.

"The other kids thought we were strange. My sister was macabre. She drew dead bodies until she became one. My brother was angry. He would scream. And I... I couldn't stand the way my classmates looked at me. The things they said. That I was a freak. They would push me down before they would let me join."

Armmie could imagine a young Alton. Then there were the other kids, faceless, and shoving young Alton onto a blacktop.

"The things they said hurt worse than the things they did," Alton cleared her throat. "It was far easier to be alone than to be in pain. And I had enough to worry about when I got home."

"You don't have to be alone anymore."

"What if I want to be?"

"I don't believe you do."

"You will have a marvelous time. Where are you off to?"

"Cairo."

"I've always been keen to visit."

"Well, maybe you should go alone instead of on the trip with people you know who are already going literally tomorrow."

Alton cracked a grin.

"Maybe."

"You don't still want me to pack all my things, do you?"

"Do you wish to continue the scholarship?"

"I would."

"Then you ought to come back."

And that was that.

Chapter Ten

Armmie laid out the details for Alton—where she would be leaving from, where she would be going, who she would be with (she not-so-secretly grimaced every time Armmie said Rocketta's name), really all the travel details. Alton gave her a stiff hug the morning she departed. That faint smell of her was intoxicating as ever, but she had to force herself to let go. The drive into London was brief and teeming with excitement. She met Rocketta at the Port of London. Rocketta had her things loaded onto the PRIVATE (yes, that's right, private) ship and then had a quick lunch before their journey.

They would take a sail across the English Channel into France, spending the night in Paris and then flying to Cairo in the morning. Armmie had very obviously never flown before, but Rocketta assured her that the PRIVATE (yes, that's right, private) plane they would take from Paris to Cairo would be a mere four and a half hours. She said they would be there just after noon.

Rocketta enveloped her in her arms and looked at her with a sentimentality Armmie craved from someone. Things with Rocketta were admittedly easier.

"And how has it been? You know I've been reading your columns religiously in the Inquirer," Rocketta doted.

"You're a flirt. I bet you have not."

"Au contraire, the most recent print, *Feathers of a Nation*, I found the analysis on the membranes of society quite astute."

So she had.

"Have you gotten up to anything else besides all that dreary reading and writing?" Rocketta asked.

Had she ever.

"Not much," Armmie said, choosing to abstain from sharing the masquerade ball that had left her an organ or two lighter, "what about you?"

Rocketta then tittered about the parties, the shopping, the "work"that her family conducted— undoubtedly evil business in the Americas—and the romance.

"He was a handsome devil... And well he was rather well endowed, but I found his conversation dreary," she said, "and couldn't offer much of a dowry."

She checked her pocket watch.

"Ah! Well, that's us, darling, we best be off."

Rocketta left a few coins on the table after Armmie tried and failed to split the check. Rocketta walked up the gangway with elegance. Armmie looked over her shoulder, as if wishing someone were...

"Do you have room for one more?" came an all too familiar voice. Rocketta looked a shade unhappy, then quashed it.

"By all means, Alton Tyner. I'll have your bags brought aboard."

The boat ride was simple, as was the train ride. Armmie never imagined in her life that she would leave England, much less travel to Paris.

Paris was beyond her wildest dreams. The craftsmanship of the buildings, the cobbled roads, the fashion! Armmie was in love with the place from the moment she stepped off the train. Alton stood off to the side as Rocketta squeezed Armmie's hand.

"The city of love?" Rocketta tested.

"I'll just have to find out," Armmie teased.

Alton just rolled her eyes and made an explosive point to carry Armmie's bag, despite there being workers to help.

They made it to the hotel only to find that there were two beds. Which certainly would have been fine if there were two people. But now, a sleeping arrangement had to be decided.

"How should we...?" Armmie began.

"I'd prefer to sleep alone," said Alton.

Rocketta grinned.

"Fine by me."

The view of the Eiffel Tower was one to behold. They could see much of the city from their suite.

"Let us get dressed for dinner," Rocketta said sweetly.

"You've made a dinner reservation?" Armmie asked.

"Darling, I've made reservations every night. Except for one day, which I have dedicated to spontaneity." Rocketta smiled. "Now, turn around and let me zip your dress. I see it's the one I bought you last time we enjoyed each other's company."

"I happen to love it," Armmie confessed.

"I love it too," she said with a wink.

Alton was holding back a scowl. She, of course, looked exceptional this evening in a teal three-piece suit and a light orange button-up shirt.

"Alton, you look sharp," Rocketta said. Alton tipped an imaginary hat.

"Sharp?" Alton murmured when Rocketta turned away.

Rocketta held open the door for Armmie and Alton, at which point she linked arms with both of them.

At dinner, Rocketta was the picture of elegance and class; she chattered, she asked questions, she was so amiable and funny it was almost hard to keep up.

"How is your research, Alton?"

Alton looked almost startled to be at the center of the conversation. Rocketta was perfectly pleasant.

"It's well."

"Have you come to any conclusions?"

"Oh, I've come to some conclusions all right."

"And what are they?"

Alton wanted to be disagreeable. It was almost funny watching her want to bite. But the issue was that Rocketta was just a nice person.

"That I've taken up painting," Alton said.

Rocketta laughed.

"I would love to see them sometime!"

They finished up dinner.

"By the by, ladies, I've heard marvelous things about a speakeasy that's just down the road, and I do think we should go."

"I'd love to!" Armmie said.

"I'll stay. Good to get some rest before travel," Alton replied.

"I won't have it, Alton. You'll be coming with Armmie and me, or I'm not letting you back in the hotel room," Rocketta said, and that was that. Alton sighed.

The bar, L'Horloge Cassée, or "the Broken Clock," was behind the wall of books in the façade of a library. As soon as the trio entered, the room was rife with jazz music. A live band seamlessly played some of the most fantastic, funky songs Armmie had ever heard. Rocketta pulled them over to the bar, where she ordered them all drinks in effortless French.

"I didn't know you spoke French," commented Alton.

"There's a lot you don't know about me," Rocketta grinned.

Soon the drinks were poured, and Alton, Rocketta, and Armmie stood around a high-top table in the shape of a clock.

"So, Rocketta, will you tell us our plans for Cairo?" asked Armmie.

"Oh darling, what aren't we doing? We've got about a trillion mosques, pyramids, museums, dunes, and camels, and the most fabulous hotel you've ever seen," Rocketta tittered.

Alton somehow seemed so stern, having heard all that, but even she couldn't suppress a smile. What a fabulous itinerary.

"Shall we dance?" Rocketta asked, putting her arms out to Armmie and Alton.

Armmie clasped her hand, and Rocketta pulled her in.

"I'll join you in a moment."

"Alton, you must," Rocketta said.

"Someone will have to guard the table."

Rocketta bowed and tugged Armmie onto the dance floor. Armmie had never danced to such jazz music before, but as one could probably guess, Rocketta was a natural. She twirled and dipped her and was so thoroughly energetic that Armmie had trouble catching her breath.

Rocketta swung Armmie across her legs back and forth, even lifting her at one point.

"Rocketta! What are we doing?" Armmie panted.

"Swing dance, darling! It's all the rage in Harlem," Rocketta replied, kicking her feet and twisting her again. Out of the corner of her eye, she could see Alton scowling as much as Alton knew how. Her eyes were cold. Her lips were twitching. Her arms were crossed. Rocketta caught Armmie's eye.

"Go back to the table," she whispered in Armmie's ear.

Armmie obliged. Rocketta followed behind and then snatched Alton's hand and yanked her onto the dance floor. Alton appeared positively shocked. She was being stiff and disagreeable, as she loved to be when she dug her heels in for no reason, but Rocketta wouldn't have it. She whispered something in Alton's ear, put her hands on Alton's back, and spun her round and round. Alton seemed to scarcely believe what was happening. Armmie watched on, sipping her drink as a begrudging smile cracked on Alton's face. Despite being several, several inches shorter, Rocketta was twirling Alton around like she weighed ten pounds.

Eventually, the jazz music turned into something much slower, something soulful and legato when Rocketta gestured for Armmie to join her. Their dance faded to a sway, then Armmie realized she might be a little drunker than she thought.

Back at the hotel, Rocketta guided her to their bed while Alton watched. She wiped off Armmie's makeup with a cloth, undid her dress, put on a sleep shirt, and brought her a little glass of water.

"Drink up, silly girl, we have a whole day of travel." Rocketta smiled, then got into bed beside her.

She was lying on her side toward the nightstand, hand gripping the side for stability as the spins ravaged her head. Rocketta rubbed her back, and Armmie couldn't help but notice the simmering in

Alton's eyes, the heat on her cheeks. Alton wanted something. She watched as Rocketta petted Armmie. She didn't move a muscle, and she never took her eyes off Armmie.

In the morning, Alton announced she would head back to London. Rocketta took one look at her and laughed.

"Stop the dramatics, Tyner." She grabbed Alton's bag. "It's aging you."

Armmie could scarcely believe it. And from the looks of it, Alton couldn't either.

In the private plane, Armmie braced herself against the wall for the entire four and a half hours.

"Are we certain this is safe?" Armmie chattered.

"Positive," Rocketta said, "now look out the window."

Below were unique landscapes, towns, villages, seas, and then desert. Armmie had vertigo.

"Have you ever flown, Alton?" Armmie asked, still terrified.

"Sure," Alton said, "loads of times."

Just another thing Armmie did not know about.

By the time they got off the plane, Armmie was ready to kiss the ground. The very first thing Armmie noticed was the people's strange garb. It was long and flowing. There were headdresses of sorts, so different from the casual wear of Britain. How positively fascinating.

Their bags were loaded into a sleek black car, and the door was opened for them.

"Where to, Madam?" asked a man in one of those flowing shirts. His accent was thick and rather beautiful.

"The Grand Oasis, if you please," Rocketta said, ever the picture of politeness.

They slid into the car. The roads to the hotel were hectic and hurried; some of the roads were hardly roads at all.

"Ooh, I cannot wait to explore!" Rocketta chirped.

"Nor can I," Armmie said.

Alton was silent, looking out the window.

"What's first on the agenda?" Armmie asked.

"Well, unpack, shower, of course. I don't wish to spoil our appetites. I have a fabulous welcome dinner planned," she said. "We will be dining with the Cairenes this evening."

"Who are the Cairenes?" Armmie.

"Family friends of my father's," Rocketta replied.

"They are one of the largest producers of oil in Africa," Alton muttered.

"Yes! And they have the most marvelous home."

The hotel was something out of fiction: domed ceilings, fountains, floral arrangements twenty feet high, carved stones, and frescoes on the wall.

"This is Ali," Rocketta said, gesturing to an extremely handsome man with caramel skin, dark chocolate hair, and a perfectly manicured beard. The way he looked at her... the way she looked at him... If nothing had happened yet, it certainly would be happening soon.

"He will be our tour guide on our trip," she said. "We each have our own room in the suite, so none of that pesky bed sharing... unless you'd like."

The room itself was just as extravagant. Balconies overlooked the grounds, which included vast pools, gardens with shaped hedges, and sports courts.

"I'm in need of a little release," Rocketta whispered to Alton and Armmie. "Travel stresses me, and I haven't seen Ali in a good long while."

She turned to Ali, who grinned with white teeth. As if he could get any more handsome.

"I don't wish to be greedy, darlings, but if I could take the first ride solo..." Rocketta trailed off.

"By all means," Armmie said with a laugh.

Alton just nodded.

"Rocketta, if I may...?" Armmie started.

Rocketta nodded.

"Don't you worry about getting... pregnant?"

"Darling, I'm infertile!" Rocketta grinned. "Greatest gift I've ever been given. Now, if you'll excuse me, I'm going to put that to good use. Come, come, Ali. I'd like to show you something I learned from the Greeks."

It was for the best that Ali was wearing a long robe, so no one could see any imprints of anything. When she went to her room and the door slammed shut with a giggle, Armmie and Alton just looked at each other.

"Are you excited?" Armmie asked.

Alton shrugged.

"Alton..."

"Armmie..."

"We are already here. Let's at least have some fun."

"I am having fun."

"You look it."

"Would you like me to laugh raucously at each thing she says? Or jump for joy when she touches you?"

"Oh, so that's what this is about. Alton, there's nothing stopping you from touching me."

Alton stiffened a bit. In the faintest distance, the sound of moaning and thumping.

"You take the room closest to her."

"You wouldn't like to share a room? The space is large enough for us, that's for certain."

Alton shook her head and retreated moments later. Armmie rolled her eyes. *Oh, Alton, what am I going to do with you?* she thought.

Her room was enormous. A four-poster bed with a gauzy white canopy, a window that overlooked a pool, a sofa, a walk-in closet, a shoe rack, a private shower... it was all too much. She heard a few loud groans that she knew from experience belonged to Rocketta.

She decided to try out that gorgeous stone shower. The floor was mosaic; the steam, the shampoos were so effervescent with flowers... everything was divine. Armmie walked out of the shower and put on the fluffiest bathrobe she'd ever worn and walked into the communal area, hoping to find Rocketta.

She did, with Ali and all fourteen of his abs wrapped around the waist in a towel. Rocketta had her hair up in a towel as well, flushed.

"Armmie, I just wanted to let you know the showers are big enough for two. Or two more, depending on whether you like a tight squeeze."

"I'll keep it in mind, thank you," Armmie said.

"Ali, will we see you for our transport to the Cairenes?" Rocketta asked.

"Yes, Madam," he said.

He stood. Tall, dark, and handsome. Armmie nearly had a fit just looking at him.

"Armmie, if you'd like a turn..." Rocketta began.

"Madam, I am not a pony to be ridden," Ali said.

Rocketta leveled a glance at him, he at her, and then they both laughed.

"I'll see you all in the lobby," he said, kissing her cheek. She smacked his ass.

"Any good?" Armmie asked.

"Oh, darling, he's a stallion," Rocketta said, "but he keeps refusing citizenship. The man loves his country. And don't listen to him. He'd do anything for a beautiful woman. As would I."

She twirled a lock of Armmie's hair.

"My, I'm lucky to know you," she murmured.

"Oh, Rocketta, you flatter me."

"I don't flatter anyone, and you know it."

"What should I wear tonight?"

"Something chic. On the modest side... seeing as we will be dining with some high-brow individuals. The partying begins tomorrow."

"All right, I'll dress."

Alton came out, also in a robe, and looked cranky.

"I'm not feeling my best," Alton said, feigning illness. "I think travel does not agree with me."

Rocketta looked her over.

"Alton, come here."

Alton appeared confused, but she walked to Rocketta.

"Sit on the sofa."

Alton did. Rocketta stood over her, inches taller.

"Now tell me, Alton, why have you decided to be sour? Do you refuse to have fun on principle?"

"I'm not feeling well."

Rocketta's expression changed to something Armmie had never seen before on her face: displeasure. She snaked her hand into Alton's hair and grabbed hold at the base of her scalp, gently, but with force—an impressive display of dominance without hurting a hair on Alton's head.

"Now, I think I've been very generous, haven't I? Paying for our little vacation." Rocketta turned to Armmie. "Haven't I?"

"You have," Armmie replied.

"Haven't I, Alton?"

"Yes, you have," Alton mumbled.

Now, this was a sight to behold. Alton, obeying. Armmie never thought she would see the day.

"So you're going to be agreeable and delightful," Rocketta crooned, "or I'll send you back. Last chance, Alton. Do you want to go back?"

No reply from Alton.

"Say it, Alton."

"I don't want to go back."

Armmie's heart was positively thundering in her chest. She had never even considered doing something like this to Alton, but a whole new world of possibilities was opening before her very eyes.

"That's what I thought." Rocketta pressed a kiss to Alton's temple. "Now you be a good girl. You can be a good girl for me, can't you?"

"I can."

"Full sentences."

"I can be a good girl."

Rocketta ran her other fingers gently up Alton's prostrated neck.

"You might even have some fun. That's all I ask," Rocketta said. Then she let go of Alton's head, but held her chin in her fingers for a moment, studying Alton's beautiful face.

"I may even reward you if you deserve it. Now go get dressed in something nice."

And then she disappeared into her room. Armmie had her jaw on the floor. Alton didn't even seem to register what had just happened.

"Wow," was all Armmie could say.

"Don't you start," Alton scowled.

"Aren't you supposed to be a good girl?"

Alton stepped closer to Armmie, grabbing her by the hips and pulling her in.

"Do not think that I will behave like this for you," Alton murmured in Armmie's ear. Under ordinary circumstances, this would really work on her, but she had just learned a new trick.

"I don't think you will. I know it," Armmie murmured back. There was a moment of great tension. Who would break first? They stared into each other's eyes, each determined not to be the one to move.

"Armmie, Alton, now," came a snapping voice. Rocketta.

As requested, the trio was to die for. They looked better than their best. Alton wore an olive-green suit and a pearl silk shirt with a sage neck kerchief; Armmie in a midnight backless satin dress, and Rocketta looking like a peach chiffon fairy. Ali had his hand on Rocketta's knee the entire ride over. They pulled up outside the most absurd house Armmie had ever seen. And that's saying something. It looked more like a temple than a house, with ornate spires and domes and palm trees lining a massive pool that split the driveway in half. It was unbelievable.

"This is where I leave you," Ali said. "I will see you all tomorrow at 10 a.m. for our adventures."

"You're not coming?" Armmie asked.

"I am merely a common man," he replied.

"Uncommon in some places." Rocketta smirked, then kissed him. "See you tomorrow, Ali."

The car stopped, and Ali got out. Before Rocketta exited, she looked earnestly at Armmie.

"Armmie, darling, you know I think the world of you?" Rocketta asked. Alton stiffened.

"Yes....?"

"Then I must be honest. The people we are going to meet tonight have certain expectations about social class, which I am not fond of. Though our peers care far less, their parents... how do I say this..." Rocketta trailed off.

"You want me to pretend I'm rich?"

"That you come from money," Alton finished.

"Yes. Oh, Armmie, I'm sorry. I didn't even think of it til now," Rocketta said. She looked earnest enough.

"I understand," Armmie said.

"Please don't hate me forever," Rocketta said with pleading eyes.

"Rocketta, you brought me here. You're a lovely girl, and you treat me like a queen." Armmie smiled. "How ever could I be mad at you?"

Rocketta sighed with relief. She kissed Armmie on the cheek.

"I promise you, darling, this is the only night we must play house." Rocketta smiled. "Then the real vacation begins."

Ali knocked on the door.

"All right in there?"

Rocketta pushed out of the car to reveal the huge carved stone doors that were pulled open by two people. Out walked a stunning woman with sleek, long black hair and fantastic eyebrows.

"Wow," Armmie said.

"Wow," Alton agreed.

They had the car doors open for them, and Rocketta bounced out and swept the woman into a hug.

"Cyrus, you minx." Rocketta smiled. "What did I say about getting more good-looking!"

"That I would blind the sun," Cyrus replied.

Rocketta kissed her cheek, and they shared a quick moment. Had Rocketta been with everyone?

"Cyrus, allow me to introduce my travel companions, Armmie Charon, and Alton Von Tyner."

"Von Tyner?" Cyrus raised an eyebrow. "I was sorry to hear about your family."

Alton smiled placidly.

"Welcome, my honored guests," Cyrus announced, "follow me."

Inside was a massive atrium in a three-story sandstone building, surrounding an oasis pond with palms and flowers.

"Are those flamingos?" Armmie asked, incredulous.

"They were brought here from the south," Cyrus responded, voice like spun silk. "There is a menagerie on the grounds if you should like to see it."

Armmie thought of all the wild creatures locked in cages and decided she did not.

Cyrus led them into a dining hall where a long table covered with candles and dishes lay. At the head was an older man in a long navy shirt with gold embroidery and an older woman in a merlot gown with white embroidery. Cyrus led them over, and the man, bald with a huge beard, smiled.

"Welcome," he said, voice booming.

Armmie bowed.

"That's not necessary," said the woman.

"Armmie Charon and Alton Von Tyner, meet my mother and father, Cleo and Ra," Cyrus said.

"Thank you for welcoming us into your home," Alton said.

"I was terribly sorry to hear what happened to your family. Your father was a great man," Ra said.

Alton forced a nod. Armmie hoped this would not be a pattern.

"And you, Rocketta, you've been away too long!" said Cleo, kissing Rocketta on both cheeks

"Oh, please, don't act like you've missed me." Rocketta grinned.

"My guests, we have planned a feast this evening, before the games," said Ra.

"The games?" asked Armmie.

"Indeed," Cleo said, "we will pay five hundred pounds to the winner."

Armmie had a nearly impossible time keeping her mouth off the floor. Rich people truly were a different breed.

"What do these games consist of?" Alton asked.

But before anyone could respond, a crowd of about ten more people rushed into the hall. Hugs were passed out, and Armmie was swept into a whirlwind of introductions. It turns out Cyrus was one of a lifelong group of friends who had all grown up together. They were all tremendously attractive socialites with clear skin, flawless hair, and endless style. Ramses, Isis, Ahmed, Noor, Sahar, and their parents, Heba, Amir, Rami, Ranya, and more. Armmie didn't catch the names of some. Soon after, they were seated, down the table by Cyrus and Rocketta, but still close to Cyrus's very intimidating parents and a barrage of people who did not know that Armmie was a nobody. They all seemed very keen on Alton Von Tyner, whose parents and grandparents had made a lasting impact. Some questions included:

"Is it true your uncle killed your father?"

"Yes."

"And how did it happen?"

"He stabbed him."

"And what of your uncle?"

"He died."

"So you're all alone?"

"Yes."

"What's happened with your family businesses since they died?"

"I manage them."

"Do you miss them?"

"Terribly."

"Do you still have all the properties in Ibiza?"

"Yes."

This surprised Armmie.

"And the sailboats?"

"All gone but one."

This also surprised Armmie.

"The cars too?"

"A few remain."

"What have you done since they died?"

And this is when Alton looked at Armmie for help.

"She and I have been working together on our studies. You may have heard she received the Pioneer Award from the London Learning Society," Armmie replied.

Some near her at the table's interests were piqued. Those being Noor, Ramses, and Sahar.

"I'm sorry, could you repeat your name?" Noor asked.

"Anne Marie Charon," Armmie replied, "though I go by Armmie."

"Armmie Charon," Ramses said. "I'm not familiar with the Charons."

Yes. Well, that would be because her father was known by no one but the barkeep, and her mother had a self-induced lobotomy.

"They are a prominent family in the north of England," Alton said.

"Very close with my family," Rocketta chimed in. "Her family deals in textiles."

"Textiles?" Isis asked.

"They own many factories across Britain, but those are more passion projects by my mother," Armmie said. "My father is secondborn to Duke Alexander Charon of Wimbleshire."

Not a real person. Not a real place. Fingers crossed they didn't know their geography.

"Ah! Well, a friend of Rocketta's is a friend of ours," said Noor.

Cyrus looked over Rocketta.

"Have you chosen a tribute this year?" Cyrus asked. "Your... what was his name... Ali?"

"Oh, darling, he's fallen terribly ill," Rocketta lied, so effortlessly.

"Then you can choose one of the servants to be your champion," Ramses said.

"Who are your champions?" Armmie inquired.

"Mostly prisoners who want their freedom," Sahar said, "I know two servants of ours will be competing."

"Rocketta, you simply must have a champion," Isis said, "you swore you would this year."

"There are plenty of servants to choose from," Noor stated.

"Well, I —"

"I can do it," Alton stepped in.

Their part of the table fell silent. Soon, the other side fell silent as well. Now all eyes were on Alton.

"Surely you jest, Von Tyner," Ramses said. "There is no point for a noble to compete in a game like this. It is beneath you."

"I do not feel that way."

"Ms. Tyner—" Isis began.

"Alton is fine."

"Alton," Isis said, "the trials are... how do you say... unpleasant."

"I can handle it."

"Do you need the money?" Noor said.

"Not in the slightest," Alton said, "but I'll compete as Rocketta's champion. She can do as she pleases with the money."

"Alton, that's not necessary," Rocketta said.

"Please," Alton replied, "I'd like to repay your generosity."

Rocketta laughed. "If you aren't eliminated on the first round, the prize money is yours."

Everyone at the table seemed unsure of this arrangement, but before they could discuss the topic further, servers distributed a parade of food throughout the table. Roasted peacocks, elaborate poached dates, barracuda, lamb, honey, fluffy breads with tangy dips, and a never-ending supply of wine. At one moment, a young woman accidentally knocked over Armmie's empty glass. She shuddered and apologized profusely, looking mortified and fearful.

"It's quite all right," Armmie said. "There was nothing in the glass."

Everyone looked at Armmie, put off.

"Armmie, it's unnecessary to talk to a servant," Isis said. Then she snapped something in a language that Armmie did not understand. She did not want to show her hand—that she was a poor wretch herself, but conversely, being a poor wretch could not change her habits.

"I like to be subversive," she replied, "if you would please fill up my glass, we can forget about the whole ordeal."

The young woman bowed her head and filled Armmie's glass.

The Cairenes on her end of the table all looked at each other with a sense of potential distaste.

"Armmie Charon, you are too good for this world." Rocketta grinned. "Isn't she just?"

Isis and Noor looked at each other, deliberating.

"Indeed," Isis said. And that was that.

The conversations undulated, and Armmie learned almost too much about the Cairenes. Alton sat silent. Rocketta tittered and laughed. Eventually, Ra clapped his hands, a boom echoing through the hall.

"Let the games begin," he cheered.

Applause erupted from the table, and soon, Armmie overlooked a large pitch from constructed stands. On the pitch stood Alton and several others. These must be the servants and prisoners in question. Alton had changed into shorts and a tight, cropped shirt. The other champions were looking at her with some kind of disgust and confusion.

"What's the first game?" Armmie asked.

"It's a race," whispered Rocketta.

Ra shot off a gun into the air, and the champions took off. Alton kept a cool pace in the middle of the pack. Armmie had no idea she ran. She just assumed that Alton spent all her time reading. She disappeared into the far end of the pitch, and when the pack of runners turned and ran toward the starting line, Armmie noticed Alton pulling ahead. She crossed the line first. Armmie could see sweat dripping down her forehead and temples, the moisture peppering through her shirt. How Alton could look good even out of breath...

The games that followed made Armmie crawl out of her skin to watch. Alton held out her arm while they latched on non-venomous snakes; she walked on hot coals with her bare feet; she even held her head under water the longest. Half the battle seemed to be just withstanding the pain. Alton looked cool and only gritted her teeth, even as she and the remaining contestants faced a myriad of injury-inducing trials.

"Don't look," Rocketta whispered, and Armmie hid beneath her hands. But she kept one eye open, watching as Alton took the blows.

"How barbaric," Armmie croaked. Rocketta squeezed her knee.

Soon, it was just two left: a rugged mountain of a man named Horus and Alton.

"The ultimate challenge," Cleo said, "is archery."

"Oh, that won't be too bad," Armmie muttered. Alton miraculously didn't seem to drag, despite the torture that had occurred all evening long. Armmie shuddered to think about why.

"Well..." Rocketta started.

Two servants stood lined up against boards, opposite Horus and Alton. They both shook with fear as one of the game masters placed apples on both their shoulders and heads. Then Alton and Horus were handed bows and three arrows.

"Good luck, champions," said Ra.

One of the servants was shaking. The poor girl trembled like a leaf.

"Excuse me, Cleo, it seems that the young lady is rather afraid," Armmie commented.

"She will be okay." Cleo seemed disinterested in Armmie altogether.

"If she drops the apples even by accident, it could cause Alton to lose," Armmie said.

"Then the girl will be swiftly dealt with."

Armmie did not like the sound of that.

"I mean to ask, could I take her place?"

"And whyever would you do that?"

What would a rich person say?

"To raise the stakes," Armmie said. "Rocketta's champion having to shoot apples off the head of her dear friend? How entertaining."

Cleo raised an eyebrow.

"All right, strange girl. If you insist."

She said something to Ra, who halted the tournament.

Soon enough, Armmie was on the pitch. Fury swirled in Alton's eyes.

"What are you doing here?" she hissed.

"Don't miss," Armmie responded.

The girl and Armmie traded places, tears streaming down her face as she bowed. Hopefully, Alton was a good shot.

Alton stood yards away, brow furrowed. Horus, to her side, fired off three arrows in rapid succession, two landing and one just barely missing the man who held the apples' right eye.

Armmie kept her chin up. She leveled a gaze at Alton, who seemed to be in full concentration. Armmie nodded the slightest she could move her head without moving the apple. Alton drew the bow back, then let the arrow fly. It was all Armmie could do not to flinch, watching the arrow hurtle toward her at lethal speed. Then she felt the spray of apple juice on her left shoulder. She relaxed that side. The apple was stuck to the board behind her. She nodded again to Alton, and seconds later, the arrow pierced the apple on Armmie's right shoulder. Alton pulled the last arrow out of the quiver, the entire competition now hinging on one shot. Horus, to her side, looked on with great hesitation. Rocketta was no doubt shivering; her two travel companions were now in great danger.

Alton knocked the arrow back, Armmie sucked in a breath, and nodded again. Time seemed to slow as the sharp end of an arrow ripped through the air right at her head. She closed her eyes. *I hope she didn't miss,* was the only thought running through Armmie's head as a *CRACK* sounded above her. Armmie took a step forward, and no apple fell. All had been pinned to the board by Alton, the victor.

Cheers erupted from the stands, loudest of all from Rocketta. Alton merely put the bow down. Armmie reached her some moments later.

In the atrium, everyone gathered.

"To Alton Von Tyner," Ra said, raising his glass, "you're made of some tough stuff."

Alton nodded as everyone cheered their glasses together.

"Well, Rocketta, what shall you do with the winnings?" asked Cyrus.

"They are Alton's," Rocketta replied.

Eventually, the candles burned low, the glasses were drained, and Rocketta decided she wanted to leave. Who could argue with the Rocketta Taylor? Someone brought a car around to the front. Rocketta and Cyrus shared a tender embrace and some intense eye contact before Rocketta kissed her on the cheek and bid her farewell.

They stepped into the car after dishing out hugs to the rest of the Cairenes. When the door shut, Armmie and Alton immediately looked at Rocketta. The car rolled the massive mansion out of view.

"All right! I'm sorry! I didn't know there would be games tonight," Rocketta said. "I thought we were just going for dinner."

Armmie and Alton looked at each other.

"How are you feeling, Alton?" Armmie asked.

"I suppose a little sore." Alton shrugged.

"I'll say," Rocketta exclaimed. "Where did you learn to stomach so much pain?"

"I'm a natural," Alton replied.

"And archery?" Armmie asked.

"Practice."

"Alton, you are a strange woman." Rocketta sighed. "Say, what did you do with the winnings?"

"I gave them to the girl who knocked over Armmie's glass at dinner," Alton said.

"You did?" Armmie cried.

Alton hissed a little as she leaned back on the squishy seats of the car.

"What time is it?" Armmie asked.

Rocketta checked her pocket watch.

"Oh, it's early, darling! Only three!"

When they got back to the hotel, Alton excused herself to shower. Rocketta turned to Armmie.

"You don't think she'll hate me forever for winding us up in that situation?" Rocketta looked at Armmie with pleading eyes.

"No," Armmie answered. She really didn't think so.

"I think she's a lovely girl," Rocketta said, "quite strapping if I do say so."

"She's a tough nut to crack," Armmie said.

"I have patience, darling."

Rocketta pressed a kiss to Armmie's lips. Her lips were plump and sweet. Armmie couldn't help but kiss back. When at last she broke away, she smiled and looked Armmie over.

"I'll tell Ali to join us at noon. Goodnight."

And then Rocketta bowed to her room.

Armmie followed the sound of the running water to Alton's room. She knocked on the door, but there was no response from Alton.

"I'm coming in," Armmie said, pressing the door open. Through the billowing clouds of steam, Armmie saw Alton's back covered in harsh purple welts, her arms covered in scabs, and she sat on the floor of the shower staring numbly at the running water.

"Alton! Alton," Armmie rushed over. "Are you all right?"

"Armmie, what are you doing here?"

"I wanted to see if you were okay."

"I'm fine. Rather naked."

"I see that."

Alton stood with a wince on her raw, blistered feet and turned off the water.

"Alton, why on earth would you walk on hot coals when we have a whole city to explore?"

"It won't hurt by tomorrow."

"You shouldn't have done that."

"But a servant should?"

"That's not the point."

"I don't mind."

"It was horrible to watch."

"You made a lovely target."

Armmie wrinkled her nose.

"Alton..."

"Armmie..."

"Can I kiss you?"

"Can you get me a towel?"

"Oh. Yes."

She handed a towel to the pink Alton, who wrapped it around herself. Then Armmie looked at her with the biggest puppy-dog eyes she could muster.

"Armmie, I'm quite tired."

Armmie made her eyes impossibly bigger.

"Maybe tomorrow."

Armmie stuck out her lower lip. A little quiver.

"Oh, blast it. Okay," Alton grumbled.

She kissed Armmie. It was soft. It was humble. Armmie put a hand to Alton's face. Please never move. Alton did not listen to the voices in Armmie's head.

"Goodnight, Armmie."

"I'm coming to bed with you."

"That's not necessary."

"Then don't complain."

They got under the covers of Alton's luxurious bed.

"And don't respond to my requests for a kiss with 'blast it.'"

But Alton had turned over on her side. Whether or not she heard it, she didn't move again until morning.

The following days were whirlwinds of tours. The city of Cairo was full of limitless art, music, and people. The mosques blew Armmie's mind—the construction, the attention to detail—she understood how someone could worship in such a beautiful place. Then the pyramids.

"Feats of human nature," Ali said.

As Rocketta had pointed out, he was fond of his city. Rocketta had him in her bed three more times on the trip, generally after absurd dinners where Armmie could scarcely walk out of the restaurants. Alton had warmed up, slowly but surely, as if she realized that being a pill would only hurt herself. The trio laughed their way through the bazaars, bathhouses, and hookah lounges with beautiful women from all over the world. On the last day, Rocketta said she would see Cyrus and some of her friends for an evening at the prince's house. Armmie and Alton both declined, having had their fill of trying to impress royalty.

"You girls be good now," Rocketta said, on her way out the door after spending almost an hour deciding on which negligee to don for her endless orgy.

"Yes, ma'am," said Alton. When the door closed, Armmie looked at Alton.

"Who knew you were so obedient?" mused Armmie.

"Obedient? I'd say agreeable."

"You seem to forget 'I can be a good girl.'"

Alton scowled.

"See, agreeable."

"Why don't you be a good girl for me?"

"Oh? And do what?"

"Following along."

Secretly, Armmie had met with the concierge to plan a marvelous date for Alton. That's how they traipsed through a bustling marketplace. Armmie picked up a silver bracelet with a little cat engraved on it.

"Come here," she said to Alton, who walked over with an eyebrow raised. Armmie set some coins down on the table in front of the merchant and clasped the bracelet to Alton's wrist.

"Oh? And why a cat?"

"No reason."

Alton looked at her knowingly, but said nothing. Some moments later, however, she was clasping a necklace around Armmie's neck, taking her sweet time touching the skin at the nape of her neck. Armmie's skin prickled as she felt the presence behind her.

"We should get something for Rocketta," Armmie said. They elected a pair of cat earrings.

After a museum and a stroll by a fountain, the sun began to set. Armmie dragged Alton along to a fancy restaurant with dining on a terrace overlooking the city. They ate a tasting menu prepared by the chef and drank Egyptian wine.

"What do you think Rocketta is doing right now?" Armmie asked.

"The better question is who," Alton replied.

"Or perhaps who isn't she doing?"

"It might be a smaller list."

"You've warmed up to her, I see. Perhaps you misjudged our dear Rocketta?"

"I had no ill feelings toward her, and I don't understand why you continuously suggest that I did."

"You just mentioned our time together an awful lot for someone with no ill feelings."

"Well then, I have no ill feelings anymore."

They ate in silence for a few moments.

"So, Ms. Charon. You're about to begin your independent study period," Alton cleared her throat. "Have you chosen a topic of study?"

Oh. Right. The whole reason they even knew each other in the first place.

"Alton, I haven't the slightest."

"Well, you ought to start slighting. There's no way for you to complete the scholarship without it."

"So you're saying you don't want me to stay forever."

"I'm not saying one way or another. I'm saying that in order for you to receive the reward, you have to complete an independent study."

"And how exactly does this work? If there's no library for me to locate what books I might need, and you aren't providing them?"

"You can tell me what you want, and I will procure it."

"You're impossible."

Alton took a sip of her drink and then looked out at the city. She looked positively dashing tonight, in a navy pinstripe suit and no visible shirt underneath. Armmie had no idea what she was going to write about. But that was a problem for a future Armmie and a future Alton. All she knew was the woman in front of her, and the woman she was right now.

"Alton?"

Alton turned her head back.

"Do you love me?"

Alton looked her up and down. The moment she asked, she wished she could shove it back in her mouth. Armmie's heart rate picked up. The longer Alton didn't reply, the more insane the waiting became. She shouldn't have asked. This was a mistake. She should have moved on. What was she even doing here? Should she be with Rocketta? Just when she thought she would pass away in the endless silence—

"Yes."

Hm. Well...

"Full sentences."

"Yes, Armmie. I love you."

Armmie could just about die. It felt like a thousand fireworks were exploding in her chest every second. Her face heated. Alton just looked at her as if pretending she had done nothing revolutionary. As if she had told Armmie to wipe some food from the corner of her mouth. Armmie reached over the table and kissed Alton. Alton pulled away after a moment.

"We are at dinner, young lady."

Armmie rolled her eyes. They finished the wine. They went back to the hotel room and overlooked the ground and stared at the stars in the sky. Rocketta was nowhere to be found. In Alton's arms and lying against her chest, Armmie would have been content to watch a meteor come from the sky and smash the world to bits. Alton's arms were powerful, but her hold was gentle. Then somehow, Armmie was kissing Alton's neck. Nibbling down her collarbones. Then, somehow, they were inside. Somehow, Armmie was on top of Alton. Somehow, she was doing that thing where she whimpers and squirms and breathes Armmie's name. Then, she was somehow on top of Armmie, riding her fingers, her hair flowing past her shoulders with each bounce of her hips. Armmie felt Alton clench around her fingers as she shook violently. Armmie thrust her fingers, and then for some reason, the door swung open, revealing Rocketta.

"How dare you!" she cried.

Alton and Armmie, both nude, looked at Rocketta with wide eyes.

"I have been waiting for this the whole trip, and you started without me?" Rocketta exclaimed. "Shameful, both of you. Get off her, Alton. I'm going to show you something you've never even considered."

"Alton, play with me," she instructed.

She got on her hands and knees, arching her back in Alton's face while she leaned in to kiss Armmie. As they kissed, Armmie could feel the vibrations of pleasure in Rocketta's lips on her own. There was a moment when she knew Alton was inside Rocketta because her lips parted and she moaned into Armmie's mouth. Her breaths were shorter as she dragged Armmie's bottom lip through her teeth, then kissed down Armmie's stomach before stopping between her thighs. Armmie watched as Alton thrust into Rocketta, and she couldn't deny that the sight of it was doing crazy things. How Rocketta's ass could be that voluptuous but her waist so small... well, it was a gift to them all.

Then Rocketta decided she was bored.

"Armmie, we are going to trade places," she announced, then lay back in the spot where Armmie had been. She put her fingers in Alton's mouth, who moistened them, and then she guided Armmie on top, but facing away from her. Alton lay at the base of Rocketta's feet while Armmie put her face between her legs and slowly teased her tongue along the wetness that had pooled. Then Rocketta started bouncing her hands up and into Armmie, who couldn't help but delight in the curling motion of Rocketta's fingers.

"Now you know what to do with Alton, don't you?" Rocketta said.

"She's very proficient," Alton said, snaking her fingers into Armmie's hair and pulling.

Armmie tried to say something, but it just turned into an *oh*.

It grew somewhat challenging to concentrate on the task at hand, what with Rocketta stroking the inside of her, but she felt a flash of delight as she realized she could give and receive concurrently. Alton's hands were in her hair, pushing her face in, while Rocketta scratched and smacked her ass. She was in heaven.

Alton's moans were growing louder as Armmie kept flicking and caressing her tongue. Meanwhile, Rocketta took her other hand and started rubbing little circles on her clit while she fingered. The woman was a menace in the bedroom, and soon Armmie was gasping on Alton as Rocketta made her orgasm fiercely. Alton finished soon after. They were all panting, then Rocketta cleared her throat.

"I believe I am owed some special attention," she said, "Alton, I'll take your tongue, and Armmie, I'll have your fingers."

Needless to say, Rocketta was right. Neither of them had considered this before.

…

The flight home from Cairo was somewhat mournful, what with the realities setting in. Of course, Rocketta had three more vacations lined up, all of which Alton and Armmie were more than welcome to join her on. She emphasized this multiple times, but Armmie had an independent study or something. Rocketta kissed her on the mouth while Phillip loaded their trunks into the car. Alton looked off into the distance.

"Alton," Rocketta barked. Alton snapped to attention.

"You listen to me, and you listen good." Rocketta looked her dead in the face. "If you do not make this girl the happiest in the world, I will land my plane on your front lawn and do it myself. Are we clear?"

"Rocketta, that's hardly necessary." Armmie laughed.

"We are clear, Rocketta," Alton replied. Then Rocketta kissed Alton on the cheek.

"You're a good soul," she said, "both of you are. Now get out of here, or I'm kidnapping you and taking you to Montenegro."

Armmie and Alton got in the back of Phillips's car and watched as the waving Rocketta grew small in the rear-view mirror.

Chapter Eleven

Armmie toiled on the subject for her independent studies for over a week after her vacation. Alton was clearly doing her best not to shrink immediately after their luxurious trip. Something about this house made her crawl back into herself; it seemed to Armmie. For the life of her, Armmie could not figure out why. At one point or another, she came to her epiphany.

"I've figured it out," Armmie said to Alton at breakfast. Alton wore a relaxed pair of trousers, loafers, and a cashmere sweater.

"And that is?"

"Why rich people are crazy."

Alton laughed.

"Seriously?"

"Seriously."

"You're not interested in the history of the Khartiliaks? The downfall of the Tome Empire? Onizan's The Great Divide?"

"While all of that is fascinating, I think I've decided."

"And whatever inspired this?"

"What do you think it was, Alton? If you had to guess?"

"Was it me?"

"Not quite. No, I'd say it was all the lavish homes I've visited, the private transport I've taken, the jewels I've worn, the parties I've attended, and their unbelievable debauchery." Armmie sipped her tea. "I hate to say it, Alton, but you people are crazy. And I intend to figure out why."

"Hm."

"Does that behoove you?"

"It's your independent study, Armmie. By all means, do with it what you please."

"You'll have to bring me books."

"So I will."

"I'd like the history of money to start. Where it began, in what civilizations and first applications and known uses," Armmie said. "And how long must this paper be exactly?"

"Forty-eight pages."

"Forty-eight pages?"

"Twelve weeks, times two reports, times two pages. Simple math, really."

"And I'm supposed to present you a fifty-page paper all at once?" Armmie asked.

"Two pages at a time. Keep up, Armmie," Alton replied.

Armmie rolled her eyes.

Research was fairly smooth after she got started. Alton kept her word in getting books for Armmie, and the paper began to shape. Once one had nothing to work for, money lost its meaning. Then, one loses the ability to want. You do not yearn for something you could have at any given moment. You want what you cannot have, or what you have to toil to achieve. It is the wanting that derives the pleasure, not the thing. If there is no wanting, then itches never really itch because the scratch is so immediate. The itch's stakes continually increase, hoping the scratch will finally make the person feel satisfied. If one could buy every jewel in the world, what was so special about them? Soon, she came to her conclusion: money causes madness.

It seemed more or less that Alton was following along. She didn't come up with any massive objections, or if she had, she kept them to herself. Things between the pair had markedly improved since Cairo. The winter trudged on, with Alton finally making an effort—it seems Rocketta's threat had worked. There were candlelit dinners, and there was dancing. Armmie was so in love. She almost didn't want to ruin it. Almost. But she knew that there was something that still had to be done.

Armmie stood at the end of the aged hall, staring down the maroon doors like a bull about to charge her. Alton had gone to town for a book that Armmie asked for that Alton could not find. The reason why she could not find *A Complete History of the Shekel* was that it didn't exist. It felt wrong to deceive Alton. It felt like she was trying to spit out hot tar that kept sticking to her tongue. There was no other way to get Alton out of the house, and Armmie had sincerely tried.

One step at a time, the doors loomed closer into view. Her breath caught in her throat as she reached them. There were those worn handles that Alton had no doubt gripped hundreds of times. She put her hand on the handle and pressed down, but of course it was locked. Armmie had hoped it would not be, but she had come prepared this time with a thick piece of cardstock. She slid it in between the doors, jimmied it, and clicked. The doors glided open so slowly, and Armmie's chest was thundering. She exhaled sharply and walked inside.

The lights were off, but the lamps illuminated a large dark mass in the hallway. This was certainly the library, indeed two stories, with silhouetted books and shelves that ran up to a domed ceiling. She found a light switch by the door and flicked it on. A large white sheet covered the thing in the center of the room.

Heart thundering now, Armmie stepped with great trepidation toward it. Each instant brought intensity Armmie could hardly stand. Her throat was dry. She could scarcely breathe. What was under the cloth that Armmie was so forbidden from seeing? With shaking hands, she pulled the sheet off.

She gasped, all the air escaping her lungs in an instant. What she beheld was inconceivable.

Under the sheet was a dais, upon which sat five chairs. In four of those chairs were the preserved bodies of those who could only be Gregory, Eloise, George, and Annie. There was Alton's taxidermied family, frozen in time. Those who had once been living, breathing people were now rendered into porcelain dolls. The poor children were so young. George, with brown curly hair, glass eyes opened as if he were afraid even in death. Annie, neat as a pin, with dark sunken circles and lines around her mouth, despite only reaching twelve. She looked so old to have died so young.

And Alton's parents were monstrous. A long beard and no lips on her father, his bald head shone like a waxed floor. He had a scowl permanently etched on his face, and his fists were huge. Her mother, Eloise, was the definition of pinched. Her mouth, her frown, her glossy eyes. It seemed like at any moment she would snap awake, screech like a banshee, reach out her gnarled nails, and yank on Armmie's hair.

Their skin was sallow and gray, but their likeness was perfectly preserved. Whoever had done this knew the family intimately. Their glass eyes seemed to stare right at her, haunting, demanding why she was in the library, why she had come.

She had to get out of here.

Armmie turned to the door to rush out and yelped aloud to see Alton, who looked as ghastly as her family.

"I told you to stay away," Alton whispered.

"Alton, I—"

"I told you. I *told* you."

Alton started to shake.

"And you *didn't listen*, Armmie! *You had to do what you want!*" Alton started screaming and gasping simultaneously. The woman Armmie loved had lost control of herself.

"You don't listen. YOU NEVER..." Alton fell to her knees, chest heaving. "Get out! Get out of my house!"

"Alton—"

"GO! GO! GET AWAY." Alton looked at Armmie with inhuman rage. Alton's life-perfected poise and composure, her mask, shattered.

"I—"

Alton stood up in a flash, face turning red.

"Leave now, Armmie Charon. I never want to see your fucking face again," Alton seethed, storming over.

Armmie stood frozen. Her heart skipped a beat. Alton's teeth were gritted so hard, her jaw so tight, that her head was vibrating. Her fists were clenched so furiously that her knuckles were turning white.

"I'll kill you. I'll—I'll do it if you don't LEAVE RIGHT FUCKING NOW!" Alton was now inches from Armmie's face.

A few tears ran down Armmie's cheek. Her throat burned. Alton looked furious. She must hate her.

"Fine."

She turned on her heel and walked out the maroon doors. She got about halfway down the hall when she turned around to see Alton on her hands and knees. Armmie had never heard such cries. Such angry, bitter tears. Such bile and sadness. Alton. The woman she loved, using her own elbows to prop herself up so as not to collapse on the floor. Armmie watched for a moment, stomach churning. Her heart ached for the poor girl. Keeping her family here? Had she taken an unburdened breath in all these years? Oh Alton. Sweet Alton.

Armmie stood back over Alton, who had curled into a ball before she changed her mind. Alton realized Armmie had returned. She snapped to her feet, her fury returning in an instant.

"I thought I told you to get out, Charon!"

"No."

Alton's chest rose and fell as if her heart was giving out. Her menacing stance seemed to tower over Armmie. Yet now, Armmie didn't care.

"You'd better go," Alton hissed, her breath now hot on Armmie's face.

"I won't."

"I don't want you here! I want you gone!"

"I don't care."

For a fraction of a second, Alton's eyes softened. Her face was still red, still vibrating.

"What do you mean you don't care?"

"I mean, I don't care that you want me gone. And I don't care about whatever is happening here. You aren't... doing anything to them, are you?"

"What? *No!*"

"Okay. Then I don't care."

"But it's insane."

"It's okay."

Armmie reached out a hand and very carefully touched Alton's cheek.

"Tell me what happened."

Something shifted drastically in Alton's face. The redness faded. Her jaw unclenched. Her eyes, no longer taut with anger, seemed to water a little. Then tears spilled over her cheeks.

"My parents arranged the whole thing. They wanted to live here forever, and they… they… it was my siblings first and they… and they've been sitting here for… for… for fifteen years, and then my… my parents after… and… and… and," Alton choked out before she could not speak through the shuddering cries. Armmie wrapped her arms around Alton as she sobbed and sobbed.

"Ple-please don't j-j-judge me," Alton cried into Armmie's neck.

"You aren't responsible for it one bit."

That only made Alton cry harder. But Armmie rubbed her back in big circles. Eventually, the tears did not come, but Alton could still barely take in air.

"Breathe with me," Armmie said. And she counted big breaths off, the two sucking in air and blowing it out in tandem.

They were downstairs some time later, Armmie having made some tea for Alton as she petted her head.

"Would you really never have shown me?"

Alton nodded.

"You could have told me," Armmie said.

"I didn't know how you would respond. I couldn't stand to... lose someone else."

"You won't, Alton. I'm not going anywhere."

They lay in silence for a long time. Then Alton sat up.

"Do you feel better now?"

"I've been carrying that for a very long time."

Armmie kissed Alton so softly, barely perceptible.

"I know."

Alton looked at Armmie for a drawn moment.

"I love you."

"I love you too."

"But—"

"But?"

"You broke my one rule."

"I'm sorry."

"As such, I must remind you that per our agreement, there will be consequences."

"Alton! You cannot be serious. Now?"

"Yes, Ms. Charon. Please go to your room, and I will meet you there."

"This is ridiculous. Surely it can wait till tomorr—"

"Now, Ms. Charon."

There was that tone of voice again. She had rebounded from a full-blown meltdown to headmistress in a matter of moments. It was impossible to argue with her.

Armmie sat in her room with her legs crossed on the sofa. Whatever was Alton going to do? Hopefully, this would not be a continuation of her "I'm going to kill you" threat. And hopefully that rage was gone for good. Armmie twiddled her thumbs, listening to the fire crackle, when she heard a knock on the door.

"Come in," Armmie said, heart now thundering for a second time today.

Alton came in looking entirely refreshed, as if nothing out of the ordinary had happened this evening. She strode in and sat in a chair across from Armmie, not saying anything.

"Yes?"

"Ms. Charon, I feel I have been pretty lenient when it comes to your stay here."

"Plus or minus a few things."

"I must once again emphasize that you were presented with one rule. Which was..."

Armmie said nothing.

"Go on. You're a smart girl. Remind us."

"I was not to enter the maroon doors."

"And what did you do?"

"Alton! Is this really necessary?"

"I'm waiting."

Armmie groaned.

"I opened the maroon doors."

"And why did you do this?"

"Because you never would have shown me on your own."

"Be that as it may, we must address your disobedience."

"Okay... so address it."

"Ms. Charon, stand up."

Armmie was admittedly a little nervous. She stood.

"Come here."

Armmie stood by Alton.

"Bend over my knee."

"Alton. Please."

"That's Ms. Tyner to you. Now don't make me wait," Alton ordered, rolling up her sleeves.

This entire front was so ridiculous and yet so tantalizing. Had she opened the maroon doors for this? No. Had Armmie been fantasizing about this moment since Alton mentioned it in the kitchen ten months ago? Maybe.

Armmie knew that if she said in earnest to Alton she did not want to, Alton would let the whole thing go. But she had a lingering suspicion that would leave both of them deeply unsatisfied. While Armmie continued her deliberations, Alton grabbed her by the wrist and gracefully laid Armmie over her lap.

Now her head was facing the floor, and her whole derriere was exposed. Alton placed her left hand on the small of Armmie's back, holding her in place and absolutely torturing her. Couldn't she just start already? A rather intense sensation had returned between Armmie's legs, and Alton hadn't even done anything yet. Oh, the humiliation... *oh, the humiliation...*

Armmie noticed something firm and almost cylindrical pressing into her stomach, but before she could question it further, Alton's hand swung down and hit her ass. Armmie gasped a little. She couldn't believe this was happening. Again. There was one issue. Armmie's skirt was in the way. It seemed she and Alton shared the thought at the same time, because she could feel Alton's fingers working Armmie's skirt up when she cursed under her breath.

"Armmie Charon, you naughty girl," Alton said, running her fingers up and down Armmie's bare legs. She wasn't wearing any underwear.

"Sorry, Ms. Tyner," Armmie said sweetly.

"You will be."

Well, they both knew that wasn't true. But it seemed Alton was determined to try. A few more smacks had Armmie's toes curled. The feeling of skin on skin. The faint sting. Alton was not being gentle. And Armmie could not be more grateful.

Never in Armmie's wildest dreams would she have come up with a scenario such as this. She wanted to be embarrassed for all the whimpers and gasps that filled the space between the harsh slapping, but she was too busy dripping down her own thighs. Alton did not seem tired out in the slightest. After several minutes—if not hours—of Alton's careful and varied strikes, she stopped. Armmie couldn't say she was glad for it.

Armmie turned her head over her shoulder to look at Alton, who was looking down at her. Oh, she was perfect.

"Have you learned your lesson, Ms. Charon?"

Had she?

"There aren't any more maroon doors for me to open, Ms. Tyner."

"I didn't think so."

Alton stood Armmie up, not bothering to adjust her skirt.

"Go get your hairbrush," Alton said.

"What?" Armmie exclaimed.

"I won't be repeating myself." Alton leveled a glance at her. Armmie tried to pull her skirt down.

"Ah, ah. There's no need for that, Ms. Charon."

Armmie returned moments later, the front and back of her lower half throbbing in a way that made Armmie crave release. She bent back over Alton's lap. There again was the firm cylinder in Alton's pants pressing into her abdomen.

Alton held the brush against Armmie's ass. It was cold, smooth wood, a little larger than a fist.

"What do you think it's going to take to prove to you the importance of obedience?"

"I don't think there's a number in the world that could do that."

Crack. Wrong answer.

"Ten?"

"That's a lowball, Ms. Charon." Alton raised the brush again. "Let's say fifteen. You remember your manners, don't you?"

"Yes, Ms. Tyner."

"Good girl."

That aching need in her core just about reached a peak as Alton brought down the hairbrush. Armmie let out a combination of a moan and a grunt. It was certainly more painful than her hand.

"You hit like a girl," Armmie said with a smirk.

Crack. Now there it was. That hurt just right.

"I'm waiting, Ms. Charon."

"One. Thank you, Ms. Tyner."

Crack. Armmie gasped. Wow. Wow.

"Two. Thank you, Ms. Tyner."

She waited for three, but instead felt Alton switch the brush between hands and pressed two fingers inside Armmie. She slid right in. A deep moan tumbled from Armmie's lips.

Crack.

"Three. T-thank you, Ms. Tyner."

It was almost too much. Yet Alton managed to gracefully walk that line between pain and pleasure as she pumped her fingers inside Armmie again and again in rapid succession with the blows from the brush. Armmie was gripping Alton's thigh for dear life by nine. By twelve, her ass was starting to really sting, but she couldn't quite even focus on it because of what Alton was doing with her other hand. By fourteen, she was on the verge of climax.

"Fi-f-fteeen, t-hank yo-u, Ms. Ty-ynerrr," Armmie moaned as she came all over Alton's fingers. She shook like a mess. Alton's fingers did not stop until Armmie lay still and limp over her knee. She pulled her fingers out and put them in front of Armmie.

"Suck them."

Armmie was in no position to argue. She sucked herself off Alton's fingers. She didn't taste as good as Alton. She stood Armmie up.

"You did very well, Ms. Charon."

"Thank you, Ms. Tyner." Armmie was doing her absolute best to regain composure, but Alton did not make it easy. Her knees wobbled. Alton stood, once again reminding Armmie of the height difference. She wrapped her arms around Armmie. It felt so good to be in her embrace. Armmie could stay there, could die in those—

"Get on the bed, Armmie."

"Huh?"

"Go."

Once again, no position to argue. Armmie got on top of the covers. Alton approached her. She effortlessly undid the buttons on Armmie's shirt and slid off her skirt, leaving her nude. She got on top of Armmie, who immediately unbuttoned Alton's shirt. *At least play fair.* Armmie shucked off Alton's shirt, furiously kissing her now. Armmie went to unzip Alton's pants when out came that odd cylinder. It resembled a cock. But it was decidedly not real.

"What's that?" Armmie panted between kisses.

"Your best friend."

Alton spread Armmie's legs with her own and pressed the thing right to Armmie's entrance. Armmie instantly knew it was going to be huge.

"You're going to take this like a good girl, aren't you?"

"Yes," Armmie whispered back.

"Do you want me to be gentle?" Alton breathed in her ear, gnawing on the lobe.

"Maybe?"

"Too bad."

And then she pushed herself inside. The size shocked Armmie. It filled her up. She was so full of Alton. It felt as if someone looked in her mouth, they would be able to see the tip. But the stretching, the infernal stretching, was nothing compared to the fucking. The thrusts of Alton's hips were powerful; the consistent slamming shook Armmie's whole body. Armmie was learning so many new things about herself. Principally, that she loved Alton and everything she did. The noises coming from Armmie's mouth were short of yells. Oh, it felt so good.

Alton, Alton, Alton, oh Alton, oh my god, Alton.

"God's not here," Alton murmured, "you pray to me."

A whole new wave of pleasure shivered through Armmie's body. Then Alton pulled out in an instant. Before she had a second to question, Alton had put her hands on Armmie and flipped her onto her stomach.

"Hands and knees, princess."

Armmie barely had a moment to pick up her hips before Alton was pressing her lower back to arch Armmie for her. She was so exposed. Alton wrapped her hands around her hips and guided herself back into Armmie. As if it could even be possible, Alton was even bigger from behind. She fucked Armmie like it was her last night on earth. She was hollowing Armmie out. Finally. Armmie had been craving this for months. The slam of Alton's hips on the recently tenderized skin of Armmie's ass brought her close to tears.

"You're mine, Charon. All. Mine." Each word punctuated a thrust.

Yes, I'm yours, I'm yours, I'm yours.

She shuddered as another climax rippled through her that came out of nowhere, but Alton kept driving her hips forward until she was satisfied. Eventually, after Armmie and Alton had completely spent themselves, Alton removed herself from Armmie and wrapped Armmie in her arms. They lay entwined for long moments, Alton holding Armmie, when Armmie felt jolts coming from Alton. And little moans. She was touching herself.

"Do you want...?"

"Don't move," Alton said.

She held Armmie tight with one arm. Alton was very ambidextrous, to her credit, and came some moments later, sinking her teeth into Armmie's shoulder. When she finished, Alton could hardly believe what had just occurred.

"Did you really just do that to me?" Armmie whispered.

"Did you really just let me do that to you?" Alton whispered back.

Armmie breathed a chuckle. Yes. With fervor, in fact. Armmie slept in Alton's arms that night, dreamless and content.

...

"Losing one's connection to desire takes away from what it means to be human. For whatever reason, our brains flood us with pleasure when we do something kind. When we treat one with care, when a friend is nice, we feel good. These things are free. There is no cost to kindness. No fee for charity. Money, in many ways, alters your connection to pleasure. It skews it. Somehow, things, objects become well... the object of desire. The increasing supposed value of an object is so arbitrary. Would a rabbit consider a diamond valuable? Or would it think of a diamond as an odd rock? In *Monster Money* by Martin Carrawack, the author describes this phenomenon: 'when your whole life is wrapped up in stacks of coin or pieces of paper, a righteous mountain looks pointless without your name on the top.' Instead of seeing beauty, money makes us crave ownership."

Armmie turned to a room of aristocrats from the London Learning Society. "Though I hardly need to tell you all. The point is not that one should burn all their money or give it away in droves—though the droves thought is worth consideration—but rather, remember that skewing desire does no good for one's head. Money won't cure madness. It is the very cause. By never working, by always wanting, you will never feel satisfied because you will not have earned what you have. But there is a better kind of fulfillment, that of kindness. In all, remember that the things that feel pure, that feel honest, the true pleasure you receive when you do goodness... nothing is worth more than that."

A moment of silence from the audience. Armmie gulped. Uh oh. Did they not appreciate her work? Perhaps telling a room full of rich people their money made them crazy was not in her best interest. Then, applause. The longer her words lingered, the more they seemed to resonate. Alton stood in the back, wearing her hair in a twist and wearing a crimson sweater, nodded at Armmie in approval.

"You mean to suggest that there are ways to feel pleasure outside of spending or receiving money?" Jasper asked, some time later.

"It might even feel better," Armmie said.

Jasper nodded thoughtfully. "You'll let me run your paper, of course?" he asked.

"Of course," Armmie replied.

"Good show!" he said. "You've given me something to think about."

Rocketta approached Armmie, immediately engulfing her in a ravenous hug.

"Congratulations to the newest member of the London Learning Society," Rocketta said mid-squeeze.

"I can scarcely believe they said yes," Armmie confided.

"Well, I'm certain a sponsorship from the chair of the board helped." Rocketta let go. "Not that you don't deserve it a thousand times over."

"You're too sweet."

"Just how you like me."

"It was wonderful of you to stop by for our winter ball," Armmie said.

"Any opportunity to get you and Tyner alone."

"You'll have to come visit in Prague."

"Oh! When do you move, darling?"

"The end of the month. I'm starting in the spring semester."

"Armmie, I couldn't be more thrilled for you if I tried. Properties out there can't be too much, can they?"

"I wouldn't know. Mr. Bonaparte pays handsomely, but not that handsomely."

"Well, darling, we will be sad to see you go." Rocketta leaned in again. "She's been treating you...?"

"Like I deserve," Armmie finished her sentence.

What Rocketta didn't need to know were the gritty details: the fine wine and elegant dinners were one thing, but the drawer of ... toys she and Alton had been accruing would make any gods-fearing citizen blush. Not Rocketta, of course, because she likely had a flogger tipped in gold, but that was beside the point.

"I'm thrilled to hear it." Rocketta kissed her cheek. "If you two are going steady, then I won't kiss you in front of her. Unless we are behind closed doors…"

Armmie felt a familiar hand on her shoulder.

"Your discretion is appreciated, Ms. Taylor," Alton grinned.

"You're a flirt, Tyner," Rocketta replied.

"Get lost." Armmie kissed her back on the cheek. "Come round before I go?"

Rocketta bowed and drifted off into the crowd of milling and bumbling Londonites. Alton placed her hand on Armmie's lower back.

"I'm very proud of you," Alton said.

"Will you show me how proud you are?"

"If you can wait till we get home."

Armmie opened her mouth to argue—

"Don't you whine, Ms. Charon. It's unbecoming."

"I'll be coming—"

Alton crossed her arms.

"So the talk was all right?" Armmie changed the subject.

"Better than you rehearsed."

"Phew."

"Are you ready to become a learned woman?"

"As if reading one hundred books in a year didn't make me learned?"

"Now you'll be prepared for your degree."

"Your tutelage was invaluable."

"What big words you're using."

"You're impossible."

"I'm possible. Now go mingle with your new socialites. I'm sure they have burning questions for our most recent member."

"I'm starved, Alton. I want dinner."

"I'll take you to a fabulous restaurant after this." Alton squeezed her rear. "And then I'll have you for dessert."

Armmie attempted to remain unflustered, but her reflection in one of the hall's many mirrors said otherwise.

That night, Armmie treated Alton to dinner for her birthday. Alton had tried desperately to keep it hush-hush so as not to draw attention to herself on the day of Armmie's talk, which she appreciated to an extent, but that didn't stop her from sharing the information with a few members of the London Learning Society.

"Why are we sitting at such a large table if it's just the two of us?" Alton asked.

"Well..."

"Because darling, we weren't going to just let you celebrate your birthday alone," said Rocketta in

Alton's ear. Alton seemed startled, as startled as Alton could ever seem. Behind her were Jasper, Reginald, and Cornelius.

"What are you all doing here?" Alton asked.

"I'd celebrate the day my dog died if it meant I could drink myself silly," Cornelius said. "Now think about what I'd like to do with a happy occasion."

They all pulled out seats at the table.

"But I thought you all didn't like me," Alton said.

"Well. We have seen the error of our ways," said Jasper.

"We'd like to sincerely apologize, Tyner, if you'll have us," said Reginald, pouring some of Alton's wine for himself.

Alton looked at Armmie. Armmie shrugged. Alton looked at Rocketta. Rocketta grinned.

"Oh, what the hell," Alton said, "forgiven."

They cheered to Alton, and then for her birthday, everyone took turns seeing who could give her the best orgasm.

Some days later, Armmie and Alton stood in the cemetery in front of four tombstones. Armmie had the good sense to slip Greary some bills and ask that he, with the utmost discretion, facilitate the removal of four statues and place them under their respective tombstones. Greary nodded without a word. Alton was polite enough to pretend as if she was unmoved either way. But Armmie knew by the way Alton stared at the gaping space in the library that all she felt was relief.

"Would you like to say a few words?" Armmie asked, slipping her gloved hands into Alton's.

Fresh snow had fallen the night before, now covering the mounds of dug dirt where the pair stood.

"No."

"Alton."

"Armmie."

"Don't be ridiculous."

"Oh, fine." Alton exhaled sharply. "Family is fickle. I'm sorry to my siblings. To Georgie and Annie. I tried everything I could to save you. I ripped my nails off trying to claw through the doors the nights you both died. I wish I could have seen you grow, but I'm glad I get to see you rest. And to my parents... what a waste. I spent my whole life hating you. I was freed when you died. But I hope you all wait in peace until I join you."

Armmie squeezed her hand.

"Do you really want to be buried here?"

"I want to be cremated."

Armie couldn't help but snort.

"That was beautiful, Alton."

"Thank you... for doing this."

Of course. She would do anything for Alton. She would give everything she had.

"Don't mention it."

Alton looked at her, something in her eyes. A look of surprising sweetness, of honesty and peace. She looked like she was going to say something so profound, and then leaned in to kiss Armmie.

Her mouth was soft as warm butter and sweet as honey. She could die a hundred times inside her lips every passing second. Armmie wrapped her arms around Alton's hips. Alton pulled away but remained in the embrace, her forehead resting on Armmie's. The morning air was crisp. There was no wind, but the feel of the snow caused a little shiver to run through Armmie. Or that's what she told herself. Alton sniffled hard.

"Okay."

"Okay?"

"Let's go eat breakfast."

Epilogue

The cobbled streets of Prague were even more medieval and stunning than Armmie could have possibly dreamed. The haphazard magazine she saw about the University of Prague once upon a time was a travesty of the real thing. Strange smells wafted down the narrow alleys, and the colorful banners and awnings of shops made London feel so far away. Birdsong seemed to float on the wind as Armmie collected her most recent book: *The Brief and Mystical Tale of Mick Herring,* which was the first assigned to her by an actual professor instead of Alton Von Tyner. Her heart twinged as she thought of her time with Alton. How she had loved to be curled in the reading room, to give her reports in the sitting room, the garden, and the patio. She missed the balls and the riches and the traveling and the luxury, but ultimately it was not her life. That said, her reports generated so much revenue for the *Inquirer* that Jasper now offered her one more full column. He added a tremendous bonus on the next ten as he hoped to create a "competitive offer." But the manor house... and Alton...

There was a welcome dinner for new students—a rather informal but appreciated gesture from the university. Armmie sat at a table of nervous, chattering new students, each trying to fill the space with fun facts about their hometowns and what fascinating new cinema had revolutionized the world once more.

Armmie excused herself politely to scan through the crowd. All sorts of people were here just to learn. To experience new thoughts both in the lecture halls and among each other. What a riveting time. Excitement tingled in her fingertips. She had forgotten that this year with Alton actually had been for a reason.

She made it back to her room. After fumbling the door open, she was delighted to see the fire already roaring in front of two wingback reading chairs. The faculty apartments were far nicer than the students' ones.

"How was the welcome dinner?" asked Alton, closing her book.

"Boring. And what about you, adjunct history professor?"

"Boring. My titles make me out to be a far more interesting woman than I am."

Her titles, it turned out, were a master's in theology and ancient history. Apparently, Alton had already pursued these degrees in tandem, not one year after she finished her bachelor's.

"I couldn't disagree more."

"That's because you love to disagree, Armmie Charon. Now come sit in my lap." Alton spoke. "I'm absolutely sick of being apart."

Armmie, of course, had no choice but to oblige, nestling herself in Alton's arms.

"What's the policy on teacher-student relations at this school?" Armmie asked.

"Best we not find out," Alton said, kissing Armmie furiously.

Armmie straddled her, meeting her kiss with equal ferocity. Alton's hands in her hair, dragging down her spine, aroused her in an instant. As she shifted her hips, she noticed the odd cylinder had found its way back into Alton's pants, the devil. Not that the very same cylinder hadn't found its way into a desperate, begging Alton on the very first night they moved in. Yes, she could do with a little release. First day of school jitters and all that. A few bounces here and there found her gasping Alton's name. And then they were spent. Sweat glistened on Alton's brow as she rested her head on Armmie's naked breast.

"You gave a wonderful performance," Armmie said.

"I live to serve."

Armmie gazed past Alton's perfect face into the sky that had turned to blue night. She could see bits of the stone city from Alton's room, the cathedrals, and the plazas. It was all so thrilling. What good fortune she had seen that ad for the scholarship in the paper. Had it not landed on her desk, she would have missed it all. She never would have been here, lying in bed with a formerly reclusive heiress turned part-time professor. Alton had acted as if the position had just presented itself, though Armmie suspected that Alton could become a professor on the moon if she'd like. So they'd locked up the house and piled their things for Prague. Rocketta insisted she visit within the week. It was unclear if the bed would be big enough for one more. But that was light-years away. All there was now was Armmie and Alton and Alton and Armmie over and over in her head until she fell asleep.

Acknowledgements

Thank you to my marvelous partner. I've tried writing this acknowledgment to you a hundred times and each time I fail to capture just how I feel about you. You have made my little life on this Earth profound. Words can't describe how I love you, but I'll spend my life trying.

Thank you to Parker for being the first person to read this book and encouraging me to get it out there. It would still be on my computer if it wasn't for you.

To Immy Grace for treating this book with such care and polishing everything. Sorry if I left behind any typos.

Caroline, thank you for making such a fabulous cover. You made it easy to judge this book by it.

Even though it's a gay smut book, thank you to my mom and dad for supporting me on this journey. I couldn't have done it without your help.

And to you, dear reader. I hope you have enjoyed and are ready for the next one.